THE SHIPYARD

THE VOYAGES OF

BRIAN SEA-WORTHY

An Historical Adventure on Lake Champlain

THE VOYAGES OF BRIAN SEAWORTHY

by *Ralph Nading Hill*

ILLUSTRATED BY
ROBERT A. BOYAJIAN

Vermont Life Magazine and
The Vermont Historical Society

FOREWORD

So accustomed have we become to change, that the past is beginning to seem more remarkable than the future. Only four decades ago it was still possible to travel almost all of the way from Vermont to New York City by steamboat. From beyond the threshold of Space, that era already seems light years away.

In *Sidewheeler Saga* I tried to recapture the bright epoch of the great white steamers of eastern lakes, rivers, and sounds, yet had the feeling that meaningful material unsuited to nonfiction was slipping through my fingers. There is more to history than the marshalling of facts. Indeed, fiction may better portray such intangibles as human values and the spirit of the times. While there are limits beyond which the novelist trespasses upon history—when, for example, he trifles with the life of an historical figure by inventing something he is not recorded as having said or done—no such restraint applies to a fictional character in an historical setting.

In this book the people and principal boats are imaginary, but the background and all details of life afloat on Lake Champlain and the Hudson River a century ago are authentic.

R.N.H.

vii

To my nephew
and
abiding friend

**RICHARD
SHAW**

The Voyages of BRIAN SEAWORTHY

CHAPTER

Wherein Parson Bugbee

Bears Grievous Tidings

And a Stranger Appears

THE SHIPYARD NESTLED IN A COVE near the end of a peninsula which the Indians called *Quineaska*, or Long Point. Life there was half ashore and half afloat and nary a complaint from any local boy was ever heard. Beyond the store-houses were apple orchards and fields of wild strawberries and barns pungent with hay and horses. When winter quilted the woods, deer took refuge in the birch and alder thicket behind the carpenter shop. High water brought pickerel and bullpout into the wooded swamp on the western shore. In summer small-mouth bass hid in the shadows under the rafts of logs chained together in the Harbor.

Below the sawmill with its coughing steam engine lay the wharf where the shipyard tender, *Gloria*, always tied up. After the ice went out in April and the big boats steamed away, the *Gloria* had the Harbor all to herself.

1

Launched shortly after the death of my mother, for whom she was named, she proved a worthy memorial as the sun caught the gold lettering on her pilot house and turned the steam from her whistle into a glittering coronet.

My grandfather, Jahaziel Seaworthy, remembered when Lake Champlain sailing packets were the principal means of passage between Canada and the United States, and he was present at the launching of the first woodburner. He said her captain sprinkled gunpowder through her hull ready to touch off should she fall into the hands of the British during the War of 1812. I never knew my grandfather. He was over fifty when Father was born, but the gunpowder incident can be taken as gospel because Grandfather was a no-nonsense Yankee, and Father, who passed the story on to me, wasn't given to exaggeration either. If I had written down everything Father told me that Grandfather had told him, our memories of the great white sidewheelers and the men who ran them would encompass a century.

I came to regret that Father protected me as he had; one or two summers afloat as a waiter or scullion might have helped compensate for my youth in shouldering the burden that became mine. As the mascot of the shipyard I had inevitably become somewhat spoiled; even in the one-room school I was looked upon rather as an heir-apparent. But I walked as far as the other students to get there and strove to cut my share of wood for the hungry stove which glowed like a winter sunset.

It was on such a frigid day through a patch of window not frosted over that I saw Agatha, Parson Bugbee's sway-backed mare, approaching at a faster pace than usual. The Parson, as everyone called Henry Bugbee, would deliver a sermon to a needy congregation at a moment's notice. He was as much an expert on colonial history as on the Bible, and on summer excursions to historic places he could usually be found on deck lecturing about the battles there. He was short and wide amidships, like a trimming barrel, and his neck was lost under his double

2

Brian Seaworthy

chin which shook when he emphasized a dramatic point. On the rare occasions when he lost his temper, he could be as volatile as Old Bess, the machine shop boiler.

The sleigh stopped in front of the schoolhouse door. The Parson emerged from under his buffalo robe and entered, speaking in low tones to Mr. Lampwood, the schoolmaster. From the pale, doleful look on the Parson's face when Mr. Lampwood motioned to me, I had a dreadful premonition that the worst had happened—we were rarely dismissed from school under other circumstances.

The Parson said very little until we had turned around and were out of sight of the school. Then we stopped and in a monotone intended to disguise his own apparent anguish, he said, "You know, Brian, this is a beautiful frosty morning and you're a fine strong young man who can stand almost anything that can happen. Your father has had an accident and I want to come to the point. The Lord has seen fit to open the great gates to him and say: 'My son, your work on earth is done . . .' "

3

This was the premonition I had had. But to accept it as truth seemed an utter impossibility.

The next few minutes were the most desolate of my life. I cried out loud and cried silently until my mittens were soaked. At length the Parson, his own eyes full of tears, said, "Your heart, and mine, are torn and bleeding, but remember, God knows best. Your father rests in an eternal place not made with hands." He rapped the horse with the reins. "Now we will go over to your home." Then, realizing I no longer had anyone to go home to except Mrs. Mayberry, the housekeeper, he added, "This will not be easy. But you will be the man to do manly things as they come to you to be done. Never forget that, though unseen, God is ever present."

I could not see how God could be ever present and take from me the only parent I had ever known. We rode on in a silence broken only by the crunch of hooves and sleigh runners and the distant booming of the ice on the lake as it froze deeper and pressed harder against the rocky shores.

By the time we reached the shipyard, I had learned that Father had gone quickly and without great pain. A steam pipe had burst in the boiler room of the new Hudson River boat whose design and construction he had been supervising in New York. The steamer's chief engineer had died also and his assistant was badly burned. A flange improperly bolted had caused the explosion.

I was spared, two days later, the four-and-a-half-mile journey to the railroad station and, not being the strong young man the Parson told me I was, would have preferred not to attend the funeral either. I was grateful that I did, for the service was almost as inspiring as it was solemn. The Parson spoke of how Grandfather had started with nothing and how he and Father, on a land-locked lake far removed from great tidewater ports, had made their steamers, and their officers and crews, whom they dressed in uniforms, models of neatness and order. Famous travelers had indeed testified that in grace and elegance no other steamers in the world were their equal. The gathering in the old cemetery was in uniform—captains, engineers, pursers, mates, deckhands—nearly everyone I had heard of who had ever worked for Father. These people were Yankees whose heritage dictated that displays of emotion were not merely unfashionable but a sign of weakness. Yet when the Parson spoke the last words of the prayer, I could not discover a dry eye. How I found the strength to avoid breaking down again I shall never know.

On the way home the Parson and Captain Hawley assured me I would soon be able to fill Father's shoes and need not feel inadequate in the meantime. I said nothing, for I was too numb to feel anything, much less speculate about the future. But there seemed to be no question that Captains Hawley and Bullard, and Engineers Barnaby and DuFour could run the boats, as could Mr. McGettrick the office, with one arm tied behind their backs. The problem was my youth. Assuming I remembered everything I had ever heard about the operation of steamboats, and could apply what I had learned, how could I expect middle-aged men to accept the leadership of a fifteen-year-old who had never shaved?

So that I would not be alone, Mrs. Mayberry had invited the Parson and my good friend, Barney Barnaby, for supper. The Parson's mission now was to bind up the wound and he even forced me to smile a little by suggesting that we take the *Republic* out in the spring, I steering, Barney running the engine, and the Parson shoveling coal.

"A three-man crew for a thousand-ton boat? How would we land?" Barney wanted to know.

"Why," said the Parson, "I'd just close the furnace doors, run up the ladder, and handle the ropes!"

"You wouldn't close the doors if you didn't want to bust the boilers," grinned Barney, "and after shovelin' two or three tons of coal, you'd never make it up the ladder!"

"Maybe the pilot house would fit my silhouette better," decided the Parson, pulling down his black waistcoat which tended to rise up over his collar. "Did you know I could take the *Republic* around the

Point inside the reef? Captain Hawley said you line up Rock Dunder and Juniper Island until there's just room between 'em for a load of hay, then turn!"

"Has Captain Bullard heard about this short-cut?" asked Barney.

"Merciful Heavens, no! Perish the thought!" exclaimed the Parson, his double chin shaking. This gave him an opportunity to imitate Captain Bullard: "My dear Parson, your knowledge of history is without doubt sound and your judgment on the affairs of the Hereafter credible, but you had better not waste your time on navigation, let alone such barnyard navigation as that."

"I'll bet he never heard of packin' the seacocks with horse manure. That's barnyard engineerin', but they won't freeze!" exclaimed Barney, whose father was half farmer and half boatman.

By the time they left I felt better. Barney and I saw eye to eye on everything, which is to say we had lived boats and talked boats since we were children. He was going to be an engineer and had already put in two years under his father in the boiler room of the *Republic*. How I wished that I too were seventeen with even the experience he had had, and the assurance that this experience had given him. He knew what he knew and he knew what he did not know. I was an armchair sailor who had heard a lot, none of which had been tempered by experience.

I gradually became reconciled to Father's death in the days that followed but grew more and more uneasy, for I knew I was going to have to call on someone for help and had only one relative, an uncle, my mother's brother, to whom I could possibly turn. Since he had never visited the Point, I knew little about him except what Father had told me—that he had been a successful businessman in Pennsylvania. My rising expectations can therefore be imagined when Uncle Reuel wrote he was coming for a visit. Someone had sent him a newspaper account of the funeral. His heart went out to me, he said, and he was anxious to help any way he could.

The importance of a relative at

hand empowered to make decisions was well understood, and on the afternoon I brought Uncle Reuel from the train, heads at the Point turned as if they were on swivels. In his overcoat with fur collar he looked like a city dweller making a modest concession to a north-country winter. But there was nothing fragile in his appearance. He was of medium height with a solid frame, ruddy complexion, a prominent chin and piercing eyes of greyish green. Since he did not know me well enough to be intimate and I did not dare to ask him his plans, the conversation on the way from the station was a little strained.

Mrs. Mayberry broke the ice. "We hope you're going to stay for a while?" she said, at the same time asking and forcing the question uppermost in our minds.

"As long as I'm needed," said Uncle. "If I am needed."

"Oh yes, very much!" I blurted out.

"My dear boy," he said, putting his arm around my shoulder, "there's nothing in the life of an aging widower that can't wait."

We left him in his room to unpack. So relieved had I begun to feel that I ran down the stairs two at a time. If Mrs. Mayberry was unhappy at the prospect of another mouth to feed, she did not show it. Indeed, when I came around the corner I saw her arranging her hair before the kitchen mirror. Brown, with touches of grey, and gathered back in a knot, it softened the few wrinkles in her pleasant face. Despite many hard years with a drunken husband, now departed, and the responsibility of bringing up her two children, she was not yet matronly. She could not have missed Uncle Reuel's remark that he was an aging widower, and appeared to be making a modest reassessment of her own future.

Was it possible that an outlook so bleak without Father could now seem hopeful? Nothing had yet been said to Uncle Reuel about the shipyard, but I was confident he would help me manage things until I could get my sea legs. The boats had never been more prosperous or in better condition, and the people necessary to run them were at hand.

Brian Seaworthy

I ran down to the long wharf where the great white *Republic* and *Bennington*, inside a field of jumbled ice, hovered over the *Gloria* and the small launches and sailboats like Arctic waterfowl over their broods. Mounting the *Republic's* gangplank, I climbed from the cross deck to her forward promenade, then up the ladder to her snowy bridge. How cold and still she was. Not a sound; none of the little noises she made even on a calm summer night as she rose and fell imperceptibly at her dock. The pilot house was full of flies which would miraculously revive in the spring. Was there anything with less life than a steamboat laid up for the winter? Or, for that matter, anything livelier in summer with her flags flying and her massive wheels thrusting a thousand passengers along at eighteen knots?

Walking the length of the hurricane deck, I descended to the afterpromenade, entered the stateroom hall and, for old times' sake, slid down the banister of the stairs to the recess. The engine and boiler rooms were colder than the air outside, "as cold," Barney's father liked to say, "as the north side of a January tombstone by starlight." Not a speck of rust was to be found on the brightwork which Barney and his father kept covered with whale oil. One of my earliest memories when tall enough to peer over the half-door to the engine room was the startling clang of the bright brass bell and the sturdy figure of Barney's father opening and closing the valves as the great piston began to rise and fall.

Ever since Father first allowed me to sit on the pilot house stool while, with bell pulls and jingler, he put the *Republic's* thousand tons next to a dock without as much as scraping the piling, I knew this was to be my life. Not just because it was his and Grandfather's but because by comparison every other must be so tame. While I was not yet old enough to assert myself in most matters, one thing was certain: I would never be anchored to my schoolroom desk when the hoarse whistles of the *Bennington* and *Republic* announced their departure in the spring.

CHAPTER

*Afloat in an Inferno—
The Second Trip Proves
At Least One Too Many*

THERE COULD BE NO SORRIER SUB-
stitute for my warm hair mattress
at home than a hammock on the
Republic. Her fo'c'sle was colder
than the shipyard ice house. Barney's kick from the bottom hammock and his command: "Hit the
deck, mate!" awakened me to my
suffering. Uncoiling myself from
my pitiful wad of blankets, I peered
out the porthole. The Green
Mountains were purple and pink
and the nearby field of ice showed
as many colors to the rising sun as
the chandelier in the stateroom
hall. The great white floes out in
the bay were beginning to move in
a fresh south wind. It was high
time; we had been waiting twenty-
four hours with a full crew except
for the assistant engineer, one fireman, and some of the kitchen help.

Barney had just started a fire in
the stove, and I decided not to dis-
turb the ice in the top of the pitcher
to wash my face. The eight deck

11

hands looked nearer dead than alive in their hammocks which ran fore and aft inside the forepeak. Ours, running athwartships in a separate compartment beside the bulkhead to the blower room, may have been a degree warmer. Perhaps I should have been a waiter, whose quarters in the stern adjoined the kitchen and absorbed the left-over warmth of the cooking range.

Stumbling up out of the fo'c'sle and over the frosty cross deck I dropped down into the boiler room just as Barney touched off the kindling in the four fireboxes. "I quit," I said. "It's too cold!"

"By noon," said Barney, "you'll wish you was at the North Pole. Go get some of Gussie's coffee." I climbed the steel ladder out of the boiler room and descended the wooden one aft of the engine to the spacious kitchen; we never called it a galley. There were bona fide portholes in the *Republic*'s hull but the stateroom windows with their common sashes were windows to us, and the hatchway stairs not ladders, but stairs. We called things as they were. Father always

12

Brian Seaworthy

thought the Navy's trouble with nomenclature arose from a desire to prove they were all old salts.

With its cheerful aromas of freshly ground coffee and homemade bread, the kitchen was our favorite refuge. The crew of a steamboat is always hungry and Gussie's passion was to keep everyone filled to the brim. The stewards never could restrain her because she had worked for the Company longer than any of them —how long even she did not exactly know. She was quite short, slight, and wiry with wisps of white hair floating about her lined face and with blue eyes to match the faded apron and worn bedroom slippers in which she padded around among her pots and pans.

"Well!" said Gussie. "How does it feel bein' up with the roosters?"

"I don't feel anything yet," I said, pouring coffee out of the heavy pot on the range. Gussie's smile revealed the gap in her teeth.

"You set down over there and I'll line your ribs in a jiffy." She gave me a little push toward the crew's table, though in past years I had always eaten with the officers.

"I haven't time," I protested.

"Oh yes you have. Barney said we won't have steam for two hours." In a twinkling she produced sausage and johnny cake and, to my delight, a slice of fresh apple pie, her specialty as pastry cook. Since there were as yet no passengers to make pastry for, she was helping feed the crew.

"How'd you get out of school to go boatin'?"

"Worked nights and took my examinations in advance."

Gussie shook her finger at me. "Your father wouldn't let you start in no boiler room, Brian Seaworthy!" There was no disputing that; she knew Father as well as I did, and Grandfather before him. I didn't care to explain that if Father had been alive it would have been unnecessary to try to prove I was an adult.

I was just finishing my pie when the heavy footfall of Captain Bullard sounded down the stairs from the dining room. He paused at the bottom, his shoulders slanted back to counteract the weight of a paunch so large that his coat would

not meet in the center. He said nothing at first but glanced around the kitchen as if expecting to find something amiss. I stood up.

"Good morning, Augusta. Good morning, Brian. Where is the cook? Where are the scullions? I want everyone fed as soon as possible." Crossing the room he ran his finger over the pastry shelf.

"That ain't dust, Cap'n, that's flour. I've been makin' pies."

"And some has already been eaten," said the Captain, observing my plate.

"Brian didn't ask for it, I give it to him."

"I won't tolerate indiscriminate feeding at all hours. The bills in this department have been enormous." The Captain turned to me. "You are not to expect any favors —no more consideration nor any less than the other firemen. Is that clear?" I nodded. "Very well." Then, starting toward the stairs, he looked at his watch at the end of a long gold chain looped around his midriff. "The Chief Engineer, Purser and I will have breakfast in thirty minutes." Gussie's nose was twitching, an unfailing sign of an-

noyance and of her poor opinion of the Captain. She seldom hesitated to answer him back. Occasionally she had contradicted even Father, but he considered that her tireless devotion to the kitchen and the welfare of the crew more than compensated for her obstinacy.

Neither his unpopularity with the crew nor the conviction of the pilots that he was a poor navigator mattered to Captain Bullard. When the ledgers were added at the end of the year it was usually his boat that had made the most money. For this reason Uncle Reuel, whose business experience had sharpened his eye for profits, had shifted Captain Bullard to the *Republic*. Since Barney's father would work only for Captain Hawley, he had gone to the *Bennington*, which left Barney on his own for the first time firing for Chief DuFour on the *Republic*.

On my return to the boiler room, the fires were well along. The *Republic* was the first steamer on the lake to burn hard pea coal, the first with boilers side by side, and with four fireboxes all in a row. The *Bennington* and her predecessors had one boiler on each side of the main deck, the theory being that if they blew up they would take only half the boat with them. Father insisted that low-pressure boilers properly taken care of would last as long as the boat, and placed the *Republic*'s in the hull amidships, thus lowering her center of gravity and improving her stability.

My first lesson was how to spread the coal evenly with no humps. "If you're too heavy-handed," Barney cautioned, "the coal won't all burn and you'll have a thick fire to overhaul." I was to know the agony of that task soon enough. As Barney tapped the water gauge on the port boiler, he remembered his father doing the same and telling him every day for a week what not to forget. "Don't forget to watch these gauges. Don't forget to blow 'em out with steam three or four times a day. On a calm day if the water in the glass don't rise and fall an inch or two as the boat moves, the gauge is plugged with scale. When she rolls in rough weather, carry two-thirds of a glass to make sure water always covers the crown sheets.

"Don't fire cold boilers too fast or you'll have steam on top and ice water on the bottom and maybe a crack in the shell. Open the firebox doors and turn off the blower at every landin'. If you don't there'll be seventy-five pounds of steam before you can say 'Cap'n Bullard!' If he hears the safety valve he'll stuff your head in the firebox for wastin' coal. And the Chief won't interfere because he's new on this boat and ain't too sure of himself. Father'd tell old Bullard to drag his pod out of the engine department and stay out!"

We had twenty-five pounds, half of what we needed, when the handle-bar moustache of Chief Du-Four appeared over the firehole. "When you have some steam?"

"Don't worry, Chief," Barney grinned. "When we do you'll be the first to get it!" It was a little early for the Chief to start his auxiliaries and he hung over the railing watching my awkward performance with the shovel.

"You t'ink you make a fireman out of Brian?"

"Sure, when he gets a little more beef on his shoulders. You think you make an assistant engineer out of me?" Barney smoothed his unruly blond hair as if this would make him a more likely candidate.

"I let you warm her up some time," said the Chief, walking around the railing and squinting at the fires.

The *Republic*'s running pressure of fifty-two pounds was reached half an hour later. Since we were standing by, Barney suggested I go up to watch the proceedings. During the winter the boats were firmly tied to the two piers with a network of two-inch lines which the deckhands were now removing and coiling "with the sun" in the bow and quarters. Although an open channel was always maintained around the boats to protect them from the pressure of the ice, a heavy band of ice farther out separated us from the open bay. To cut through it with enough momentum so that the south wind wouldn't catch us before we cleared the Harbor, the pilot needed everything the Chief could give him.

The whistle blew three deep blasts. The gangplank rumbled over the cross deck and the breast lines were let go. The brass bell in the engine room clanged twice in quick succession. Full astern. The Chief moved the shiny starting bar forward and aft. Rushing steam filled first the top of the five-foot cylinder, then the bottom. As the great piston plunged and rose, ice could be heard thumping against the paddle buckets and breaking against the stern with an ominous rumbling. The thick connecting rod propelled the massive crank and towering wheels faster and faster; now they swept the *Republic* backward at a momentum the ice could never resist.

The rumbling ceased, the stop bell rang. We had reached open water in the middle of the bay and were swinging around, stern into the wind. Now the ahead bell rang. Again the Chief resorted to the starting bar, until he could put the engine on her own. As he opened the throttle, the *Republic* surged forward to the quickening breath of the mighty engine until the dial showed twenty-five revolutions a minute. At thirty-one turns she was capable of twenty knots and was thus faster than anything on the lake and perhaps on the Hudson and the Sound. If the time ever came when I was allowed to handle her engine, I wondered whether I would have the nerve to try. I was dreaming. I had not even started as a fireman.

The hill on which Burlington rises affords an outlook to the shipyard three miles south across the bay, and the arrival of the first steamer was as auspicious a sign of spring as the park's first crocus. Factory whistles began blowing and people appeared in their windows waving handkerchiefs before we even approached the breakwater. The thumping of the paddle buckets against occasional ice cakes must have been heard a mile away, so we need not have announced our arrival with our whistle.

Melting snow from the mountains having raised the lake almost to the surface of the old Salt Dock, trimming barrels had to be rolled to port to bring the guard down so that the pitch of the gangplank was not so steep. From the moment we tied up until we sailed for Plattsburg four hours later, bedlam

could not have been busier than the gangways, cross deck, dock house and narrow passageway through the piles of freight along the pier. Coal had to be taken on first, for the boats were laid up with empty bunkers in the fall, and in the spring just enough was transferred from the coal barge at the shipyard for the trip to the city. The great black pile at the end of the railroad siding on the pier was hardly dented by the thirty tons that the deckhands now rolled aboard in a ninety-minute procession of two-wheeled carts and emptied into the bunkers through manholes on the cross deck. Amidst the shouts of roustabouts and shipping agents, six carloads of freight were stowed on the cross deck and in both gangways back to the paddleshaft. The remainder, perhaps twice as much more, was due to be picked up by the *Bennington* soon after we sailed. Room was somehow found for two carriages and their horses, but not for several cows that came trundling down the hill just before we cast off. Last aboard were the passengers: ladies in silk, old men with canes, infants in arms, and

drummers with carpet bags who had postponed their visits across the lake to avoid a tedious winter journey around the northern end by train and stage.

The two hundred seventy-five tons that Barney guessed we had taken aboard settled the *Republic* fifteen inches by the bow so that she was now drawing seven feet, the maximum permitted by some of the shallow way landings. To reach them our boats (and those of the other lakes, bays, and sounds) had evolved a rounded hull, almost flat amidships, with the deck sponsoned out on each side and with the outboard paddlewheels drawing no more than the hull. Unlike Midwestern river boats which seemed to us ungainly barges, ours with draughts almost as shallow, were fast, stable, and as slick as a trout.

The wheels as we left the harbor were ploughing deep under our heavy load and throwing chunks of ice against the paddleboxes with crashes that sounded as if we were striking rocks. By the time we reached Plattsburg, had unloaded and loaded, and ploughed our way

back in the stiff south wind, I understood what Barney meant when he said he quit every night for the first week he fired for his father. We had to handle every shovelful of the two-and-a-half tons an hour the *Republic* burned at full throttle, and some of it twice, if the ashes are taken into account. I say we handled it—I did what I could but the brunt fell on Barney's sturdy frame. At five-foot-ten he was little taller than I and not much heavier but he was much more smoothly coordinated and by making every move count, easily compensated for my deficiencies. The spring schedule had always called for three seasoned firemen; in summer on line run four were necessary, two on duty and two off. But Barney was sure that Captain Bullard, partly to save wages and partly to work Barney so hard he would quit and thus he would be rid of both Barnabys, had no intention of adding the third fireman.

Since early morning the two of us had shoveled eight tons of coal, enough, it seemed to me, to steam up the whole world. Even Barney thought we were using too much for this amount of running and that the trouble was with the coal. We had started with clean boilers and had carefully tended the fires, but they were already growing thick with impurities that wouldn't burn. Never had I craved cold water as I did now. But I would rather have had stomach cramps than drink the oatmeal water the kitchen stewed up for the firemen. Gussie happily substituted a bucket of ginger water which not only slaked my thirst but seemed to restore my spirits.

About two-thirds of the way to Burlington the Chief hollered down to hold our fires, that we hadn't met the *Bennington* and that she must have had trouble. Sure enough, leaks had developed in her port boiler around some new tubes and she hadn't yet left the shipyard. The moment we landed, Uncle Reuel came aboard to talk with the Captain, who immediately decided to make another trip to Plattsburg with as much freight as we could carry.

The Chief, who wasn't consulted, called us out of the firehole, bravely declaring to the Captain and Uncle Reuel, "Another trip and by tonight I have two tired firemens!"

With my dirty face and with the shirt I had thrown on soaked through in the few seconds it took to climb the ladder, I looked so bedraggled that Uncle shook his head with alarm. "I'm all right," I assured him. "I'm just hot and dirty."

"You're asking a lot of two firemen, Captain!" declared Barney, who with sufficient provocation would have said the same to the President of the United States.

"With due respects to your nephew," the Captain advised Uncle Reuel, "we do not have two firemen. We have one with very independent ideas and another who is a greenhorn."

"He's a smart greenhorn!" declared Barney, his eyes snapping. "He's more than pulled his weight today. You want to know what's wrong in the boiler room, Cap'n? Somebody's cuttin' corners. We always had three firemen in the spring and always had coal that would burn. This stuff is so full of slag it wouldn't burn in Hell!"

Except for the narrowing of his

eyes, the Captain's face was inscrutable. "If you don't like the coal or the hours, the shore is as near as the gangplank!"

For a moment Barney stood with as contemptuous a look as I'd ever seen on his face, then flinging open the firehole gate, he backed down the ladder two rungs at a time. The Chief, frightened into silence, volunteered no opinion on the coal, nor did he pursue the matter of an extra fireman to spell us during the eight or so hours of duty that remained for us in this day and night. He just rubbed his hands together and, noticing a button which he removed from the worn sleeve of his uniform, disappeared into the donkey room. The Captain strode imperiously out onto the cross deck, ready for anyone else who cared to test his authority.

"The coal *is* bad, Uncle Reuel. It's full of clinkers and the fires are getting so thick Barney says we may have to overhaul them before we get back from Plattsburg."

"I know nothing about coal. Captain Bullard is serving as general manager because he knows how to operate boats economically.

Let Barney tend to his firing and never mind what's in the coal. And I suggest you stop this foolishness before you get sick!"

"I'll only quit if Barney does!"

"In that case you may be quitting sooner than you think. And I won't be sorry."

"I don't like the Captain any better than Barney does," I protested. "He got mad at Gussie because she gave me a piece of pie for breakfast. Father always said the crew could have anything they wanted to eat."

"In past years kitchen expenses were way out of proportion. Captain Bullard is trying to plug some of the leaks so we can build a surplus against hard times."

"The crew ought to have all they want to eat. I should have something to say about it, shouldn't I, Uncle Reuel?"

"You could have had everything to say. You asked me to run the company until you were of age and to be conservator of your father's estate. I am trying to conserve it. I may not agree with everything the Captain does, but as long as he is in charge I shan't interfere."

Brian Seaworthy

Uncle's red face seemed even redder in the orange reflection of the open fireboxes. He mopped his forehead. "Don't be too proud to come home. Firing is a man's job. Fifteen is too young."

My eyes were smarting. "That's how old Barney was when he started! What he could do I can do!"

Turning away, Uncle threw up his hands. "We'll pick up the pieces later."

The last trip, as the Chief anticipated, was one too many, for me at least. On the way back from Plattsburg we lost our battle with the fires, which became so thick they nearly touched the top of the furnaces and would take no more coal. Purgatory cannot compare with the fury of removing a ton of ashes and glowing clinkers and keeping the fires going at the same time, for if they are not rebuilt in ten minutes the steam pressure falls. In less time than that, the firemen's shoes are burning if the smoking piles on the boiler room floor are not heaved overboard through the port in the hull.

Though feeling strangely light-headed, I lasted through the cleaning of the port fireboxes and had almost finished scraping up my part of the ashes when Barney said I looked paler than a ghost. He helped me up the ladder and I dropped to the deck right there, next to the firehole. I don't think I fainted—I could feel a cold sponge against my face, then I heard the scraping of shovels. For a few moments I had visions not of ashes and long-handled shovels but of my lookout in the gnarled pine over the Point and the glinting of the sun in the prisms of the Juniper Island Lighthouse.

All of a sudden I was riding the carriage of the old up-and-down saw at the carpenter shop and then we were gliding across the bay to town in the pung, Father and I, over the thick black ice. I awoke from my half-consciousness to find myself looking at the broad backside of Captain Bullard who had taken everything in on his way to the recess. The Chief helped me to my feet and, after satisfying himself I was no more than exhausted, sent me to bed. Shakily I made my way over the cross deck and through the hatch to the fo'c'sle.

Lacking even enough strength to get in my hammock, I fell heavily upon Barney's and had hardly drawn up the blanket before I was dead to the world.

CHAPTER

A Spiteful Adversary,
An Excess of Steam—
A Headlong Departure

ONE DREAM RECURRED AGAIN AND again that night and the next: the *Republic*'s boilers steaming along all by themselves without any hull, decks, engine, or passengers. Since we were always confined to the firehole and saw even less of the upper decks than of the passing shores through the portholes, the dream was not as far-fetched as it might seem. Nothing animal or vegetable requires so much attention as a hand-fired boiler; it calls for coal every few minutes, guzzles water almost as often, and constantly demands that its temperature be taken.

Sleep offered escape from this vigil but not from the lameness, so crippling on the second and third mornings that I could hardly lean over, stand straight, or pick up a shovel. I would have abandoned ship on both the fourth and fifth nights had Barney not reminded me that he had quit five times to my two—with an easier schedule and decent coal. This bolstered my ego, which he no doubt calculated it would. I quit again in the darkness of the seventh day, Sunday, when we had to get up at 3 A.M. to clean the boilers. After a week of hard running, the ashes clogging the iron flues or fire tubes had to be blown out. This required crawling into the four furnaces from which fires had been pulled just a few hours earlier, inserting a steam hose into the tubes, and blowing the soot into the rear connections.

I survived my half of the tubes but was so dismally wet and dirty and so hot after we had shoveled out the rear and center connections that I quit once and for all, or so I thought. Barney swore the worst was now over—that I would feel better after a night's sleep, or what was left of it, for this was our day off and we didn't have to get up. The *Bennington*'s firemen appeared at 6 A.M. to rebuild the fires and relieve us. So faithfully did I observe the Lord's commandment to rest on the Sabbath that I slept through Parson Bugbee's service in the dining room and did not

awake until shortly before supper. Returning to my hammock an hour later, I hardly stirred until it was time to go to work the next morning.

It wasn't will power that enabled me to survive one week, two, three, a month—it was just hanging on from day to day. The longer I lasted, the greater my confidence and the better my standing with the rest of the crew. To gain the esteem of others one must first respect himself. Although I had not entirely erased the impression that I was "playing fireman" when I didn't have to, most of the crew, even those much older, now accepted me as a full-fledged member.

I say most. Jib Wiley was the living proof that envy is the least curable of human frailties. Although now serving in the deck department, Jib had always had designs on the engine room and had served as fireman for various intervals. He would have been firing now if I had not, and there was no forgiving the interloper who had displaced him. He relished calling me "Junior," though my name was not my father's.

26

Brian Seaworthy

"Coffee's strong enough to grow hair on Junior's chest, if anythin' will!" Or, rising from the table: "Everybody get up. Here comes Junior. All right if we start eatin', Junior?"

My resentment was hard to conceal and when he saw he was getting my goat he redoubled his efforts. I got up earlier in the morning but couldn't avoid him at night. Once when I came into the fo'c'sle from the blower room he stuck his foot out, and I fell flat on my face. Barney wasn't there and nobody else dared say anything in my defense. Jib might have been younger than twenty-five. He was dark-haired with a pale face whose dour expression rarely changed. Of medium height, he had very strong arms; no one who had seen him pick up a three-hundred-pound anchor cared to tangle with him. He generally concealed a cud of tobacco in the back of his mouth, since there was a rule against chewing on board, and often he smelled of whiskey after his day off.

Despite Jib's lurking unpleasantness, the thought of quitting became less insistent; indeed, I was beginning to think I might survive. Everyone knew we were firing poor coal on a six-day, three-man schedule and that I was now doing fully half the work. Even the Captain could find no fault with the boiler room, though this did not mean he was pleased with it or ever commended us. He never commended anyone; doing well in his view was merely doing one's duty. A dutiful crew was a disciplined crew. Good discipline arose from respect for, and fear of, authority. And since the Captain was neither feared nor respected in the boiler room, our jobs, in Barney's opinion, were only as safe as the absence of an excuse to fire us. His appraisal, as it turned out, could not have been more accurate if he had used a crystal ball.

On the first morning of the summer schedule who should present himself as the third fireman but Jib. The two of us could hardly have done the work of four firemen but we only half expected the Captain to provide a third, and somehow it never occurred to us that it would be Jib.

"Cap'n says he needs a man

down here to pull fires—says Junior couldn't even pull a hen off the nest! 'Show 'em', he says, 'what a strong back can do.'"

"And a weak mind, and a big mouth!" Barney said.

"Why you yellow-headed cur! I could stuff both you and Junior up the steam chimney single-handed!"

I couldn't put up with much more of this, and could see that iron self-discipline was necessary for Barney to hold himself in check. When Jib threatened anyone in his way with the long iron hoe, Barney warned him to lay it down if he didn't want it wrapped around his neck.

The new schedule fortunately required me to work with Jib only a third of the time; it was Barney and I and Barney and he on the other two shifts. Whenever Jib launched one of his fusillades, which was every day, I deflected it with silence and a blank face, all the while imagining I was beating him up. Firing develops one's shoulders, and I was now a far likelier specimen than in the spring, though still not his match. Barney was, but he said he would

rather shovel coal than manure and wasn't anxious to start anything.

With Barney off duty and Jib due back from breakfast, I was alone in the boiler room one somber Saturday morning as we glided north into Essex on a reflection of thunderheads. When the whistle blew the steam gauge showed fifty pounds. I opened the fire doors as we passed the horseshoe nail factory on the point and reached for the blower-engine valve handle to make sure it was shut off. The reversing wheels churned white water past the fireroom porthole, the pilings protested with a scrunch, and the breast line went out. We were backing slowly to warp her in when to my astonishment the safety valve went off with a thud. It was set to blow at fifty-three pounds. The needle now showed fifty-five and was edging up. Why? I checked the valve handle which turned the long stem leading through the bunker to the blower engine: it seemed to be stuck part way open. The fires were livelier than they ought to have been with the doors open, but not unusually so.

In less than a minute, despite

the steam roaring through the safety valve, the pressure was fifty-seven and still rising. My heart began to drum like a pile driver. Running into the blower engine room, I found the flywheel driving the belt to the blower turning briskly. Hard as it was to grip the valve handle because of the extension to the boiler room, I seized it with both hands and twisted it with all my might. Still the blower turned. Fanned by the draft through the windways under the boiler room floor, the fires, even with the doors open, were building pressure faster than the safety valve could relieve it—much faster during the minute or two since the pilot finished with the engine. Again I struggled to tighten the valve, then tried in vain to kick the belt off the pulley. Moments later the pressure had risen to sixty-one pounds! At the first crack of thunder my heart leapt into my mouth; I had a horrible vision of the boilers blowing sky-high, carrying decks and passengers with them. Running into the blower room I pounded on the fo'c'sle bulkhead to awaken Barney.

"We've got sixty-one pounds and it's going up fast! I can't stop it! I can't turn off the blower!" It took Barney no more than thirty seconds to get from his hammock to the blower engine room. He couldn't turn the valve any farther either.

"The packing nut's too tight! Get the wrench!" It was missing from its usual place on the bulkhead. I ran into the boiler room to get another.

"We've got sixty-four pounds!" I hollered.

"Get the Chief! Turn on all the siphons!" yelled Barney. I gave him the wrench and hollered for the Chief and had just turned on the boiler room siphon when there was another clap of thunder. At almost the same moment Jib dropped down the ladder and we collided. He gave me a violent shove, and as I fell backwards I hit the side of my head on the bulkhead. Things happened so fast I could never remember how. Before I could get up, the needle on the steam gauge rose from 65... to 68... to 71... During these two or three dreadful minutes I seemed to be in a kind of paralysis, as in a nightmare when one can neither move nor speak. 73...75...78...81...83... At this point the Chief turned on the main siphon above and Barney finally loosened the packing nut. He had just succeeded in turning off the blower when for no apparent reason Jib struck him full in the face. When I entered the blower room, Barney was on his knees with the blood coming out of one nostril. He didn't rise but hurled himself forward, hitting Jib in the stomach with his head and carrying him back with a crash against the starboard bulkhead. I was on the point of jumping into the fray when a heavy hand on my shoulder spun me around.

"Stop right where you are!" boomed Captain Bullard.

"I found him foolin' with the blower engine, Cap'n! He ain't even on duty!" gasped Jib. "I was eatin' breakfast—you seen me, Cap'n—when the safety blowed."

"Sixty-two pounds!" called the Chief from the boiler room. He appeared in the doorway wiping his face and neck with a large red handkerchief, then began laying fresh coal on the fires to smother them briefly and further reduce the pressure.

"You're confined to the fo'-c'sle!" shouted the Captain, shaking a stubby finger at Barney. "Pack up your stuff. You'll get off at Burlington. You too," the Captain added, glaring at me.

"For what reason?" demanded Barney.

"Dereliction of duty," snapped the Captain. "Jeopardizing passengers and vessel with excessive steam pressure."

"And startin' a fight, I'll bet," said Barney, blotting up the blood from his nose with a rag.

"Also that. Get out." The Captain motioned toward the fo'c'sle.

And that was all there was to it. We stuffed our carpet bags as the rain pelted against the portholes. In ninety minutes, with the departing storm rumbling off into the east, we were standing on the dock in Burlington. Presently the whistle blew, the great wheels began to claw, and the white hull swept past us porthole by porthole. Then she was gone in the mist and swirling wake.

Barney covered his nose, though it was no longer bleeding, and his eyes too; he did not want me to notice that he could not keep the tears back. Stepping out of the slight, misty rain, we stood in the doorway of the freight shed, saying nothing, until the *Republic* disappeared in the fog. The *Bennington* wasn't due until five o'clock, so we sat on some kegs of molasses until the rain stopped, then slowly walked across the pier and up the hill to Lake Street. The rafts of Canadian logs in the slips and the masts of schooners and sloop-rigged canal boats were indistinct in the mist which, however, seemed to amplify the shouts of their crews, the occasional whistles of tugs and railroad switching engines, and the shrill grating of freight car wheels on the spurs winding among the hundreds of piles of lumber.

We entered the Sail Loft Restaurant, ordered coffee, and sat for a long time without a word. Black eyes and swollen faces were trademarks of the docks and lumber yards, but not the well-drilled crews of the steamboats, and we turned our faces toward the wall as we pondered our fate. What we said about Jib, who obviously had tightened the packing nut on the blower valve, did not become boys of proper upbringing and was better lost in the clatter of the restaurant. We stayed for over an hour, then wandered down among the wharves, eventually returning to the Salt Dock to wait for the *Bennington*, which was scheduled for a special railroad excursion as soon as she got in.

She appeared from beyond the point exactly on schedule, sweeping regally around the end of the breakwater. A few minutes later she drew swiftly up into the wind. Captain Hawley, ringing the bells himself on the bridge, looked astonished when he saw us, then smiled broadly and waved us aboard. We didn't wait for the gangplank to come ashore but leapt over the rail and made our way around the crowd to the starboard side of the engine room where Chief Barnaby was putting the starting bar in its socket.

"For the love of Moses, son, what happened!" he exclaimed, seeing our swollen faces. Motioning us into his stateroom across the gangway, he closed the door and locked it. "All right," he said, hanging up his coat with its three gold stripes. "Let's have it."

Barney began with the episode about Captain Bullard and the bad coal and I repeated my conversation with Uncle Reuel. Then Barney gave all the details leading up to the fight with Jib. If the Chief was surprised at anything we said, even at the shabby treatment we received from Captain Bullard, he didn't show it.

"I always knew he wanted to get rid of us," declared Barney, "and this proves it. We tried to make a go of it, we tried real hard, Father, but . . ." Here his voice faltered and he buried his face in his hands, the bold front he usually presented to the world completely shattered. Had I seemed to have failed in the eyes of my father, I am sure I would have done the same but I had always considered Barney indomitable.

"This ain't the end of the world; why, it's an honor to be fired by Bullard!" declared the Chief, puting one arm around Barney and the

other around me. "He don't know a boy from a belayin' pin. Or his rear end from the rudder. Nothin' you done was wrong, son. Maybe the Cap'n and I can find somethin' here for you boys."

We had worked so many weeks in the hulking shadow of Captain Bullard that I had forgotten, if I had ever known, what a happy ship was like. Everyone who heard our story on this great, friendly, whispering gallery seemed determined to restore whatever faith in human nature we had lost on the *Republic*. The Parson confessed that he found it impossible to apply Christian ethics in his dealings with Captain Bullard but thought perhaps the Creator had set him afloat as a horrid example for the rest of us. "There should be some good in the man," exclaimed the Parson, "though I confess I have yet to discover what it is!"

The posters advertising the railroad excursion billed the Parson as giving one of his celebrated historical lectures and when we rounded the southern tip of Valcour Island, the brass band accompanying the large crowd struck up *The Star*

Spangled Banner. Most of the crowd had climbed to the hurricane deck which Father had reinforced for just such occasions. From his vantage point near the walking beam on the turtle deck, the Parson was able to give full sweep to his powers of elocution. With a great range of gesture and voice, he pictured the miseries of the infant colonies under George the Third and the paralysis of the local citizenry struggling to defend the homeland against the advance of the Royal Navy and a mighty army of ten thousand Redcoats, Hessians, and Mohawks.

He described Benedict Arnold's feverish haste in felling trees to build and arm America's first fleet and how, manned by youths from the hearthsides of our verdant valleys, this fledging flotilla here in this very bay on October 11, 1776, had engaged fifty-three British vessels in the Revolution's first fateful naval battle. Sensing that to eat was unpatriotic while their ancestors were facing cannon balls and buckshot, even the youngest and hungriest of the Parson's listeners put down their picnic bas-

34

Brian Seaworthy

kets. Hourly the battle grew more sinister for the Americans as they put their grounded flagship, *Royal Savage*, to the torch, and the mortally crippled *Philadelphia* slipped beneath the waves. But nightfall brought reprieve: a mist that enabled the tattered remnants of Arnold's flotilla to steal undiscovered through the British anchorage. Then came the long chase southward as the Americans were forced to abandon their leaking ships and troop overland to the safety of Ticonderoga.

"Yet out of the ashes of defeat rose the phoenix of victory!" Here the Parson slowly raised both hands aloft as the audience followed the upward flight of the mythical bird. "The season was now too late for an invasion and the British returned to Canada. May the patriots who condemn the intrepid Arnold's later perfidy never forget that his little flotilla delayed the King's legions a whole year! May the memory of the radiant exploits of Benedict Arnold at Valcour and Saratoga never be sullied!" The Parson now called for a moment of prayer for the honored dead whose bones

rested at the bottom of the bay. The band then struck up *The Battle Hymn of the Republic* to the applause and cheers of the multitude while the Parson, his double chins quivering, bowed his head and held his hand over his heart.

No one found his oration more stirring or the great outdoors more refreshing than two unemployed firemen sitting behind the wheelhouse on the roof of the extra pilot's cabin the Captain had given us. We ate like horses, which we had never been able to do under the surveillance of Captain Bullard, and for the next two days we had the run of the whole boat. Like the colonists after Saratoga and Yorktown, we reveled in our new-found freedom.

CHAPTER

Lessons in Locomotion;

Deep on 'Dead Center';

Banished by the Captain

LONG AFTER RAILROADS WON THE race, steamboats still reigned supreme on those of our lakes where the mountains fall steeply to the water. Gaining a foothold along the ledges of Champlain's rugged shoreline proved awkward for the iron horse. Even after it finally succeeded, we continued to carry most summer passengers between New York and Montreal.

In the days before railroads, northbound travelers went by Hudson River steamer to Albany and from there by stage or canal packet to Whitehall, the southern end of navigation for large vessels on Lake Champlain. Our boats ran from Whitehall to St. Jean, Quebec, one hundred twenty-five miles to the north, where the lake narrows to become the Richelieu River, a tributary of the St. Lawrence. From St. Jean overland to Montreal was but a short distance by stage.

37

Lake George steamboats provided another route from the south through the mountains to the upper part of the village of Ticonderoga, where a small stream drains Lake George down an escarpment and into Lake Champlain. Beneath the great stone fort for which the town was named, passengers from the upper lake embarked on our northbound steamers out of Whitehall. That brawling terminal was connected by rail with Albany in Grandfather's time, but it was not until 1872, when I was fifteen, that the tracklayers began their assault on the rugged western shore toward Ticonderoga. Trains from Montreal were then running south to Rouses Point and Plattsburg, so we no longer called at St. Jean except on excursions.

Father told of a bustling wharf a few rods south of the border at Rouses Point where thousands of European immigrants who had ascended the St. Lawrence to Montreal swarmed aboard Champlain steamers from the trains, filling the air with strange accents. The traffic from east to west across the lake was just as lively, for there were no bridges in a hundred miles. Our strong box would never have been empty had it not been for competition so relentless that it was sometimes necessary to carry passengers free. The fastest boat with the lowest fares got the business and engineers were under constant pressure to produce more revolutions by tying down safety valves. With their lives in danger every second, you might expect that passengers would complain to the authorities. Not so. They gathered at the rails shouting for more speed. Father produced it not by forcing the boilers but by making improvements in design. Then our adversaries would launch a replica of our new boat and the competition would resume. Eventually they succumbed because their goal was always profits while ours was building better boats.

All this and more Uncle Reuel explained when, learning of our misfortune on the *Republic*, he appeared on the *Bennington* the following morning. He thought Captain Bullard was too hard on us and was going to tell him so. He could not believe Jib caused the trouble but would ask Captain Bullard to keep an eye on him. We must try not to think ill of the Captain; if rumors of a new opposition boat were true, we would become dependent upon his economies. Uncle wiped his face with his handkerchief like a man who was coping with about all he could manage.

There were always rumors of new competition but nothing had come of them in recent years. Such a threat in my young life seemed remote, for my own prospects had never been brighter. Captain Hawley announced that Barney and I were to remain on the *Bennington* and that two of her firemen would transfer to the *Republic*. They thought it a promotion to work in her single boiler room, while I was excited to gain responsibility for one of the *Bennington*'s two. And Barney was pleased to be back with his father. Some engineers are reluctant to share their knowledge with assistants who may someday threaten their jobs, but Chief Barnaby enjoyed making engineers out of good firemen. He was even willing to teach a fifteen-year-old (particularly one who had lost his

father) how to warm up the *Bennington*'s engine. This to me was becoming life's most alluring prospect, even more than becoming Captain. Though the vessel responds to the bells he rings and the course he steers, he does not govern the surging power of the majestic engine.

The Chief displayed his confidence in us by never entering my boiler room on the starboard guard except for a cheerful word, and by allowing Barney to warm up the engine every morning. Less than three weeks passed before he decided that I'd had my baptism by fire and that despite my youth it was time to learn the destination of the steam I was making. He spent many hours identifying every valve and pipe and explaining their functions, some of which seemed to me quite perplexing. While I accepted the fact that two inches of vacuum pulling one end of the piston equaled one pound of steam pushing the other, and that twenty-eight inches was a "perfect" vacuum, this antithesis of pressure seemed to me some kind of magic.

"Why do they call it inches instead of pounds?" I inquired one day.

"Because in a vacuum you ain't got pounds!" declared the Chief. "You got nothin'. You got less than nothin'. The less of nothin' you got, the more inches!"

"What happens if you don't have vacuum?"

"What happens! She gets hotter'n love in hayin' time, that's what happens! You'll have steam enough to boil ten thousand clams pourin' out of the hot-well clear up to the beam."

"What do you do then?"

"What do you do!" exclaimed the Chief in a tone suggesting a schoolboy ought to know the answer. "You got to start the fire pump to get water into that condenser steam. Then you'll recover your vacuum, but maybe not twenty-eight inches right away. She's cranky if she's hot and you got to play with her."

To a fledgling vertical-beam engineer there was as much sleight-of-hand in "picking up" the vacuum as in getting the crank past the center. Such talent wasn't acquired overnight. Indeed, the Chief

recalled he had been forbidden to operate the bar without help until the end of his second season, and it was another year before he ran the engine alone. One must never become confused and never hesitate; the slightest deviation from proper timing in stopping or backing could put a crimp in landing procedure, even damage the boat or wreck the dock.

As much as I had looked forward to my first morning in the engine room, I had become too conscious of a beam engineer's responsibilities to enjoy it. Barney hung over the half-door on the port side with a wide grin while the Chief, having oiled the steam and vacuum rods and the jaws of the rocker arms, took hold of the starboard bar.

"All right, take hold of that other bar." The two starting bars, fitted to a single shaft, were operated together so that all I had to do was watch and follow. Yet I was taut as a fiddler's bow and the Chief noticed my jaw was trembling.

"You're scared, son, aren't you? Well, I was too, and Barney there, with the grin, was jumpier his first

day than a hen on a hot brick!''

We began by "picking up" the vacuum, which required barring the engine over a couple of times. This called for an explanation of how to keep her off dead center when the piston and crank were at the top and bottom as shown at 12 and 6 o'clock on the crank indicator. The Chief admitted being on dead center several times in his career. The remedy was opening the door to the wheelhouse and prying her off with planks under a paddle bucket. This was no slight maneuver, for to move any part of the engine, whether by steam or by hand, was to move it all and there were many tons in the paddlewheels, in the thick shaft that drove them, in the ponderous crank and connecting rod, walking beam, piston rod, and piston.

Never taking one's eyes off the crank indicator when starting the engine was the prescription for not getting stuck on dead center. At the 3 o'clock position you lowered the bar and raised it just as the crank was passing bottom center, until it reached 9 o'clock; then you lowered it again. While you were doing this, you kept one hand on the cock to supply water to the condenser, and one eye on the vacuum gauge.

"Turn her over maybe two or three times without giving her any water," said the Chief. "The minute you see your vacuum start up you got a condenser full of steam. That's when to give her the water. Hear that? There she goes! That's not steam squealing, it's vacuum. See? Twenty-eight inches. She's ready to go."

The Chief spent the rest of the time before our departure talking about the exhaust valves, about the relief ports that afforded the escape of steam trapped in the cylinder by clumsy engineers; about the feed water controls to the boilers and the return of condenser water from the hot-well, and about the action of the eccentrics. He demonstrated how they were engaged to trip the valves automatically, which was called "dropping the hooks." I would not attempt that for a long time, though I was welcome to hold on to the bar while he did so. The wrong answer to a bell or jingler could be disastrous and I would have to absorb the bell system, the Chief said, "like salt pork does milk gravy." While learning all this, I would be "busier than the button on a backhouse door," but eventually it would all become second nature. Although I was only following the Chief's motions on the second bar, my head was pounding when the whistle blew and we got two bells and a jingler for half astern.

"Remember what I said about when to raise the bar and when to bear down?" I nodded. "In backin' it's the opposite; up at three o'clock and down at nine." We had been holding the breast line on slow astern and backing against the piling to throw the bow out. The lecture ended as the stop bell rang, and then full ahead. The crank indicator stood at just after 3 o'clock. Down on the bars. Down came the cross head and piston rod. Up. Up they went. Down. Down they came, faster. Up. Down. As the crank indicator crossed 6 o'clock on the fourth upstroke, the Chief reached for the handle governing the eccentrics and pulled it down. Kerklunk! The big engine was on

its own. As he opened the throttle, the deck beneath us surged forward with each quickening stroke of the crank until the shiny rocker arms were tripping fifty-six times a minute.

"That wasn't so hard, was it?" smiled the Chief. I shook my head, my fear having departed somewhat, but not my excitement which was running so high I was hardly fit for my shift in the boiler room.

During the six weeks of service remaining for the *Bennington* in that fateful summer, few were the moments outside the boiler room when I was not to be found taking turns on the bar with Barney. He had become so able that he was now allowed to start, stop, and back without the help either of the Chief or the assistant engineer, although one of them was always present. So able had Barney become that the "accident" at Bluff Point could never have happened, except under the circumstance ultimately found to have been responsible.

Every day from the wooded drive beneath the great hotel on a bluff north of Port Kent, three

Brian Seaworthy

horses with silver trappings and a coach with driver and footman swept onto the dock and drew up with a flourish as the gangplank went ashore. Arriving and departing passengers, often whole families with retinues of maids and nurses, filed between the deckhands at attention in their trim uniforms of white and blue. Then came a procession of steamer trunks, large and small, on two-wheeled hand carts. It was a fanciful scene, like a stage curtain tableau —the great white steamer at the dock, the greater white hotel far above, the one with its green chairs in rows on the decks and the red carpet in the stateroom hall, the other with green rockers in rows on the verandas and red carpet in the grand lounge.

Perhaps twenty people were waiting for us this August afternoon, for we were ten minutes behind schedule. As we neared the Cliff Haven dockhouse the carriage rumbled over the pier with another load, the sun glinting on the patent leather boots of the driver and footman and the wind blowing the cockades in their hats. Having an-

swered the slow bell, Barney had shut off the throttle and was waiting to disconnect the eccentrics. I had just come from my boiler room and was watching with the Chief outside the half-door to the engine room. The stop bell was a long time coming—much longer than usual—and when it did it was followed immediately with two bells in rapid succession which meant full astern, and hurry.

Strong broadside gusts tend to make a sail of a lake steamer's sidehouse. Steerage way can be lost on a slow bell, so it is important to land into the wind. From the engine room it was impossible to catch more than a glimpse of the dock, but I judged the wind was bringing us in too fast and the pilot needed to back off. Answering a bell for full astern while moving forward requires precise timing on the bar; the motion of the vessel through the water keeps the wheels and engine turning and they must be stopped and reversed at almost the same moment.

Barney quickly disengaged the eccentrics and stopped the engine. In perhaps three seconds he allowed the needle on the paddle-shaft indicator to drift to the 3 o'clock position, then he raised the bar with a strong fast thrust. This should have carried the piston over 12 o'clock dead center and overcome the inertia of the reversing wheels against the water. But it did not. The crank indicator dropped to 6 o'clock and stayed there. For a moment Barney stood motionless as if frozen to the deck. Then, since the indicator showed he was on or near bottom center, he gave the engine a burst of steam. Nothing happened. The bell again sounded with an urgent clang and at the same moment the Chief threw open the door and jumped into the engine room. His eyes were fastened not on the indicator but on the exhaust hook. It showed that the engine was really on top center, not bottom, and that nothing could be done!

Then came the crash. If the Chief and Barney had not been holding on to the bar, and I on to the door, we would have been thrown off our feet. The scrunch of splintering wood was followed by what sounded like four gunshots,

one after the other. Once more two bells sounded for full astern. The Chief hadn't for a moment taken his eye off the exhaust hook, which now moved slightly indicating that the paddlewheels had dragged the piston a little off the center. Suddenly he was able to bring the great engine to life and we backed as we'd never backed before. The stop bell did not ring until we were a considerable distance from shore. Then the whistle on the speaking tube from the pilot house blew. It was the Captain. "We hit the dock! I'm coming down."

In the gangways some of the passengers were running and others were shouting. Someone pulled the rope splice on an overhead rack which brought down a load of life preservers just as the Captain appeared.

"You have nothing to fear!" he announced without the least note of alarm in his voice, or a single grey hair out of place. "Nothing serious has happened! Go above and await instructions! We will land shortly."

By this time I was back in my boiler room off the gangway. Everything was normal. The pressure was down a little because I had opened the firebox doors, but it was slowly rising again now that we had stopped. When I returned to the engine room Barney was alone, for the Captain and the Chief had gone to inspect the guard rail where it struck the dock. Barney's face was taut and white and he was trembling all over. I helped him into the Chief's stateroom where I poured some water on a towel which he wrapped around his head.

"I'm all right," he said, lying down on the bed. "Find out what the devil happened."

The guard rail had hit the clump of five pilings at the corner of the dock and broken them like twigs. The sponsoned deck then passed over the corner of the dock which came in contact with the guard braces, snapping four of them off with sharp reports that had sounded like gunshots. The corner timbers of the dock, together with the rocks behind them for a distance of five feet, had been knocked into the lake.

We had no difficulty in landing. Except for a lump half the size of an egg on the head of one of the passengers, there were no injuries. We ordinarily stopped at Cliff Haven no more than twenty minutes, but today we stayed half an hour while the Captain determined that the deck was safe above where the braces had been broken. He and the Chief had no fault to find with each other, nor the Chief with Barney. The trouble was traced to the long shaft to the crank indicator which chose to sheer a pin just as Barney answered the bell for full astern. The engine became caught on dead center because he could not tell the position of the piston. The Chief swore he would never again allow anyone to trust the crank indicator; the position of the piston would henceforth be judged by that of the exhaust hook.

The broken pin in the indicator shaft generated more excitement in the engine department than the accident itself. The fracture seemed to Barney and me altogether too clean; the bright particles we found on the bed plate suggested it had been *filed* half way through. Recounting the circumstances of our departure from the *Republic*, we al-

most had Barney's father convinced that Jib had stolen aboard and done it. But the Chief advanced the more rational theory that the pin had developed a crack and when it broke had sheared off the particles we thought were filings.

The inquiry of Captain Bullard and Uncle Reuel (it was more like an inquisition) took place not in private but in the gangway outside the engine room where Barney and I were wiping and oiling after our return to Burlington. The Chief had explained that no one can predict when something is going to break, and that if the pin had not broken we would not have hit the dock, to which Captain Bullard replied:

"On the first day of the season you had leaky boiler tubes which you might have detected beforehand. If you were more vigilant, you might also have discovered the crack in this pin before it broke. In any case this would not have prevented a good operator from controlling the engine."

"What I like about you, Bullard," said the Chief with great forbearance, "you have such a low opinion of yourself and such a high one of everyone else."

"Gentlemen," said Uncle Reuel, "we're here to revise the schedule, to assess the damage, to estimate the time necessary for repairs . . .,"

". . . and to investigate the cause of this accident," persisted Captain Bullard.

"You've done all the investigating you're going to do on this boat!" declared Captain Hawley. "The responsibility for the accident is mine."

"A captain is always responsible," said Bullard, "and I as marine supervisor am responsible for both boats and all their personnel. I have not yet been advised who was operating the engine when this accident occurred."

Great forces were at work on Barney's face. By assuming the responsibility and covering up for his son, Barney's father would be doing himself an immense injustice. This was too painful for Barney.

"I was running it," he said, stepping out of the engine room.

"I suspected as much," said Captain Bullard. "We have not been running steamboats this sea-son, we have been running nurseries, with nearly disastrous results on two occasions. Henceforth only licensed engineers and qualified assistants will operate the engines of these boats. Furthermore, experienced firemen will take charge." The Captain turned to Uncle Reuel to solicit his approval.

"The Captain is right," said Uncle. "We have a grave responsibility for the safety of the public. This accident will put the *Bennington* out of operation for several days. We cannot afford to risk further interruptions."

The Chief opened the cabinet on the bulkhead and removed his license, which he carefully rolled up. "Long as I'm runnin' this engine department I'm hirin' my own firemen. The boys suit me fine. Ain't anybody else alive can burn the slag you've been buryin' us in." The Chief rapped his license on Captain Bullard's paunch. "Get this into your noggin: if the boys go, I go!"

"And if the Chief goes," said Captain Hawley, "so do I."

"Gentlemen, gentlemen!" protested Uncle Reuel, raising his

hands. "If we quarrel the Company will suffer. I beg you to say nothing more tonight. We must reach an agreement. I urge you captains to confer tomorrow. Meanwhile not another moment should be lost in proceeding to the shipyard. Repairs must begin in the morning."

CHAPTER

Out of Bad Comes Good;

Going South We Meet

Adventure in Whitehall

FROM CAPTAIN HAWLEY'S PAINFUL expression when he came out of the meeting the next morning we knew we were finished on the big boats—and correctly guessed why. To tie up the *Bennington* merely because we were not her firemen would have crippled the Company. Persuasion had failed and the Captain had yielded, for he had no leverage to apply other than leaving the boat himself.

Barney's father swore he was returning to the farm, then thought better of it. Even parental indignation was not as strong as his loyalty to the grey-haired Captain. Venting his frustration, the Chief declared that the stink from Captain Bullard's behavior rose "higher than the steam from a heap of warm horse doughnuts on a frosty morning."

The friction among the officers greatly disturbed Uncle Reuel, but not my departure from the boiler room. This I found hard to understand; I had done my full share of the work, and it in turn had produced shoulders to match my exertions and made me hard as the nails I wanted to chew and the tacks I could have spat out. Once again Barney and I had become victims of circumstance. Nothing that had happened was really our fault, yet here we were being cashiered like drunken deckhands.

After he had cooled off, the Chief philosophized that those who mattered knew our abilities as firemen and the rest didn't count. Though there were times in every life when one's best efforts seemed futile "as pushing feathers against the tide," nature had a way of making wrongs eventually right. Meanwhile our assignment on the *Gloria* wouldn't do us any harm; the Chief would like to have served on her himself at our age; she steamed easily and her engine was "sweet as apple cider."

Only two days were required to install temporary braces under the *Bennington*'s guard. On the third morning the ringing of the bell atop her pilot house and three

blasts from her deep whistle announced that she was off and away. The moment she departed the shipyard fell forlornly silent with only the *Gloria* at the wharf. Her leisurely sleepy trips to town and to landings too shallow for the big boats at first seemed deadly dull, but as soon as we were allowed to run her ourselves we had great fun taking turns in her little engine room or steering in her pepperbox pilot house.

A tug or tender rides more *in* the water than on it and there is a reality of wind and wave lost to the crews of larger vessels. Sometimes the lake was so smooth that the muffled chuff-chuff of the engine, the trail of steam from the whistle on her smokestack, the passing reflection of the clouds, the eddying and frothing of the wake behind us were the only proof of motion. Yet in half an hour the *Gloria* could be standing almost on end, so savage were the storms that rumbled out of the mountains. It often seemed that the next wave would carry her pilot house away. But at the last moment she would lift her bow, vindicating her reputation as both safe and adventure-some.

We didn't always take the short-est way back but closely circled rocky points and promontories and fragrant bays and coves deep in shadows of cedar or pine. Often we stopped to dive and swim, and once we boated a twenty-pound northern pike. We made sure Cap-tain Bullard and Uncle Reuel never learned where we caught it. When there were no errands for the *Gloria,* we helped at the shipyard sawmill and in our spare time an-gled for bass around the sunken wrecks along the shore of the Har-bor.

The life of a lake steamboat de-pended upon the wooden hull which even in fresh water rarely lasted over thirty years. Built of durable native oak, braced from stem to stern with a "hog frame" to coun-teract the weight amidships of boilers and engine, the hull never-theless succumbed eventually to strain and rot. Following the dis-mantling of the superstructure and the engine, which was often trans-ferred to a new boat, the seacocks were opened and the old hull set-

tled to the bottom to enter a new role as a likely fishing spot. I do not know how many hours we spent in the twilight trying to lure the suspicious black bass away from the rusty spikes and old tim-bers that tangled our lines if we fished too close.

One morning toward fall while steaming along the rocky east shore near Red Bluff Point oppo-site the shipyard, we saw twenty or thirty men piling lumber on the bank of an isolated cove called Mark's Bay. It was shielded from the northwest by a new stone pier which had been built the previous winter. A long cribwork of timbers spiked together eight feet high had been laid on top of the ice and filled with stone. In the spring the ice sank to the bottom with its heavy cargo. That was how docks were made in those days.

No one seemed to know who was building this one or why, though it was rumored to be part of the large estate of a rich eccen-tric. It remained idle for several weeks following its completion in mid-summer; then its mystery was solved. Mark's Bay was becoming a shipyard. Upon the arrival of schooners with additional supplies the workmen, soon fifty or sixty strong, transformed the piles of lumber on shore into dwellings and a boarding house for the cold months. Sheds for the carpenters appeared next; then a shop for the blacksmiths, and long ways sloping down the bank into the cove. As the great oak keelson grew its symmetrical rack of ribs, the echoes of sledgehammers resounded in the north wind clear to the Point across the water. There was no mistaking the 260-foot hull that by dint of dawn-to-dark labor presently appeared on the ways; it was the shape of a steamboat to provide the *Republic* and the *Bennington* with the opposition Uncle Reuel had been sure was coming.

Amidst lively speculation about her owners and the date of her completion, it was announced that she would indeed furnish opposition to the "old line," that a group of men from New York were prepared to invest all the money necessary to make her the fastest and finest vessel on the lake, and that she would be ready in the spring.

"Now you understand why I have worried," said Uncle Reuel one night. "It will be dog-eat-dog when we cut our rates next summer. That is why we have tried to economize."

"The new boat won't be any faster than the *Republic*," I asserted.

"Why not?"

"Because they won't put in a larger engine."

"What would prevent them?"

"A larger engine would use too much coal for the extra speed."

"Who said so?"

"Father."

Uncle shook his head. "A boat a little faster would get enough business to pay for the extra coal."

"I wouldn't want to be fireman on her if she used the coal we've been burning."

"Why?"

"It takes so much more of it to keep steam."

This was a sore subject to Uncle Reuel. "You're just repeating what Chief Barnaby says!" he snapped, his face flushing. "He don't think anyone else knows anything. He's wrong about the coal. Even if he wasn't, I wouldn't dictate to Cap-

Brian Seaworthy

tain Bullard. He's doing the best he knows how!''

Uncle had had some trying problems and I should have known better than to badger him. One of these times he might pick up and leave and that would be a calamity. He had been most attentive to the affairs of the Company and had given me security. I could hardly blame him for his rather distant manner and lack of patience; I was always asserting what Father would have said or done under such-and-such a circumstance. But Uncle was learning to make allowances for my age, and his disposition lately had taken a turn for the better.

One reason appeared to be that Mrs. Mayberry had accepted his engagement ring. This came as rather a surprise even to Mrs. Mayberry, who had told him several times that one marriage was enough. He had nevertheless continued his solicitations, saying it would please him if she would wear the ring. In accepting it she reserved the right to change her mind. She was in no hurry to decide, she confessed to me one afternoon. She had scarcely forgotten

the difficult years with her first husband. In marrying Uncle Reuel, she would be exchanging a life she knew for one she did not. Yet she was tempted. Uncle was presentable, almost distinguished looking. With his fine suits and city ways he represented an exciting life she had only read about. Though there was no arguing that life in the parlor seemed preferable to that in the kitchen, I declined to give my opinion when she asked for it. Mrs. Mayberry was a link with the past and somehow I did not care to share her with Uncle.

All our disappointments that year, and all our reversals, became secondary to the cracking of the *Bennington's* large cylinder, which laid her up nearly a fortnight in September while the new one was being cast in Hoboken. Fortunately, the weather had been mild and she was in shallow water when it happened, so she could drop anchor until the *Republic* came up to take her in tow. The Chief reported that on the way to the Harbor he was treated to a view of Captain Bullard strutting on the *Republic's* quarter deck "like a banty rooster —except no rooster with a paunch like his could stand up, let alone strut."

A loose set-screw on the paddle-shaft's heavy crank had in turn allowed the bolt on the keeper key to loosen. As it began to come out, the piston was forced down three-fourths of an inch so that it struck the filler piece between the condenser and cylinder. The thumping of the keeper key had given ample warning on the one other occasion in the Chief's experience when it had come loose. Since he had carefully checked over the crank assembly as late as the last week in August, the accident appeared so unlikely that even Captain Hawley was beginning to suspect foul play.

But how, why, and by whom? When a piece of leather heel was found in the crank pit and Jib was discovered to have had his shoes resoled just after the accident, the case was closed so far as Barney and I were concerned. Yet the questions of how and when he could have stolen aboard from the *Republic*, and why he would do this remained unanswered. In the absence of proof of this or any other explanation, some cutting remarks were passed around about the Chief's ability as an engineer. One more such unnecessary accident, Captain Bullard was heard to remark, and the Company would have no alternative but to replace the Chief—and if Captain Hawley insisted on going with him, he was not indispensable either. This, to a proud engineer with a superior reputation, was the height of injustice.

If anything good came of the accident, it was the trip to New York that became necessary in connection with the casting of the new filler piece for the cylinder. Although the foundry had some of the original drawings, the pieces of the old one were required to obtain precise measurements. They might have been sent by railroad but it was decided to take them down on the *Gloria* and bring the new piece back through the canal. Barney was needed at the shipyard and I was soon to begin school, yet we were permitted to make the trip as the *Gloria*'s crew providing we returned on the Night Line from New York the same day we

arrived. The Chief was to serve as captain and navigator. As soon as the new casting was loaded and he had attended to some other matters at Hoboken, he was to pick up a crew to replace us for the return trip.

New York had always seemed to me half a continent away, so far removed was it from the life of the lake we knew; yet it was only three hundred miles south by rail or—by lake, canal, and river—an easy and familiar voyage to the crews of local sloops and canal boats. I might have accompanied Father on one of his trips had he not thought me too young to fend for myself while he visited New York shipyards. And Barney might have gone with the Chief the previous fall had he not got into the poison ivy.

Our plan to return on one of the great overnight steamers called for suits. If Barney stood perfectly straight in the one he had inherited from his older brother, it would not pull away from his neck. I could barely get into mine, purchased over a year before, even after Mrs. Mayberry had let out the seams. But she said we needn't for a minute feel self-conscious, that we looked good enough to decorate the captain's table of any boat on the Hudson. The kind soul was up before daybreak getting breakfast so that we could take advantage of an early start in front of a cool north wind.

The stars were fading as we passed Quaker Smith Point and by the time we reached Sloop Island the tips of the Green Mountains were aflame. The large pot of black coffee simmering on the cylinder head was doing its work; the Chief, who had never quite recovered his buoyancy since the accident, seemed to become his old self.

"Did you know rattlesnakes could swim?" he asked as we passed the forbidding cliffs south of the lighthouse at Split Rock. "Sure can. They was pretty well cleaned out on the Vermont side 'til they began swimmin' over from New York in the spring. Used to shoot 'em as they come ashore. For a while the farmers made more money on rattlesnake bounties than on cows. But the state found payin' bounties so expensive you

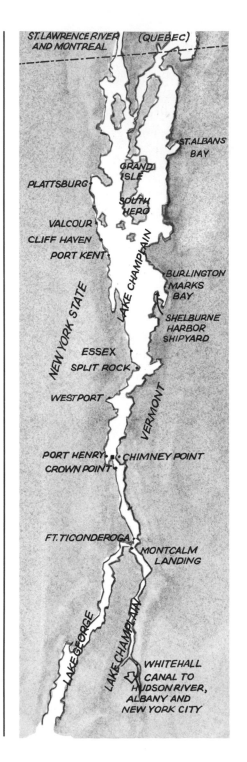

know what they done? Turned loose some wolves on the islands where the rattlers stopped on their way across. The wolves made short work of 'em by snappin' their necks before eatin' 'em. Well, sir, you know what they found a few seasons later? A new breed of wolf on the islands, every one of 'em with a rattle on the end of his tail!"

Seriously, had the Chief ever told us how Gussie saved the *Excelsior* almost exactly where the *Gloria* was now? This was the gospel truth. He was firing for Gussie's husband, then the *Excelsior*'s engineer, when flames were discovered in the woodwork around the boiler and smokestack. When the water was turned on it ruptured the hose. In the resulting confusion the fire spread rapidly. All of a sudden a huge cloud of steam enveloped the engine room and gangways and when it cleared away the fire was out. Gussie had run upstairs and aimed the stateroom hall hose through the door to the smokestack enclosure. Enough water had run down the surface of the stack and on to the hot shell of the boilers to suffocate the flames

with steam. She'd once put out a fire in the kitchen that way.

Gussie's many virtues were now given a grateful hearing. It was a long time since any of us had eaten her apple pie. I reported that she'd asked a week ago to transfer to the *Bennington*. Uncle Reuel referred her to Captain Bullard who told her she could either cook on the *Republic* or not at all.

"He's always very accommodatin'," said Barney.

The Chief took out a cigar, put it in his mouth, then removed it without lighting it, as if he were about to pass judgment on a matter long on his mind—perhaps a new theory about our multiple misfortunes. Biting off the end, he blew it out the pilot house window, which seemed to unburden him of what he might have said. Airing to the crew grievances about a superior officer is never easy; it is, in fact, mutinous.

Presently his expression brightened and he began talking about Gussie's husband under whom he learned his trade, a mountain of a man, he said, who was always cracking walnuts on the shipyard anvil with a ten-pound sledge hammer grasped at the end of the handle with one hand. Ordinarily good natured, he could bodily heave anyone who crossed him over the rail.

The wind freshened. Last night you could hang your coat on the moon; it looked to the Chief like three days of north wind and three of sun. Had we noticed the fur on the caterpillars? It would be a cold fall. Not much rain, though; the muskrat nests were low in the swamps. Kingsland Bay was a good shelter in a tight fix. Grog Harbor too. We ought to know every shoal from Bulwagga Bay to Point Aux Roches. Had we heard the Parson's speech on the forts at Crown Point? About the stone windmill where the French soldiers ground their grain? An old horse ferry with treadmills over the wheels once ran from here to Chimney Point. Another from McNeil's to Essex used six horses. We should be careful farther south where we siphoned water; the channel was crooked as an auger and we might suck up a boiler full of mud.

After five hours of steaming and five hours of talk we rounded the fort at Ticonderoga, tied up briefly to fill the bunker, and started for the Narrows. The lake, which midway in its length grandly opens into an inland sea, shrinks in the south to a channel so constricted in one place called The Elbow that the *Bennington* and *Republic* had to warp around by holding a line on shore. The Chief had never known the Narrows when it hadn't been "busier than a hen's gullet," and it was never more so than now. Other than the large steamers, lake-bound schooners and tugs, and the little "pin flats" with their single sails, scores of ninety-foot canal boats passed through every week, sloop-rigged or interspersed with two-hundred-foot barges behind tugs. So stuffed was the basin at Whitehall with hay and ore, we knew it would be morning before we got our turn at the locks.

This suited Barney and me. The toughest canal town on the continent had never known a dull moment since the hour the locks opened, and today was no exception. A tug and locomotive pulling contest, hastily arranged in a saloon the night before, was about to begin. To have arrived just in time for this seemed an act of Providence, though Whitehall was always brawling over transport. Here rail and water, steam and sail, horse and mule, Canadian, Yankee, and Yorker were all stirred up together with rum and blackstrap molasses.

A crowd even noisier than the one afloat accompanied the locomotive to the siding at the edge of the basin. Two heavy lines were passed over the bulkhead to a large tug. During the five minutes required to improvise special hitches both locomotive and tug built up extra pressure and when the signal was given, safety valves were already screeching. At first the contest seemed unfair, for the drivers of the locomotive were turning before the tug's propeller could gain purchase. While the railroaders hooted, the tug moved backward as fast as a walk. Then a curious thing happened. The wheels of the locomotive, sending forth showers of sparks against the sand sprinkled on the tracks, began to lose traction as the stern of the tug settled deeper, its propeller churning the water to a froth.

For a few moments it looked as though the losers would be the heavy lines of hemp stretched tight as piano strings. Then a roar went up from the boating fraternity. The locomotive began to give ground, slowly at first, then faster, until the tug was hauling it backward as rudely as if it were a toy. It was all over. Pandemonium reigned. As the engineer amidships doffed his cap and spat tobacco juice over the rail, the captain blew the tug's whistle. The boisterous crowd then drifted slowly away to the bars on the main street along the canal above the basin.

In the evening we went ashore for the sights but all we saw was confusion under the dim lanterns of the waterfront. Much of it was generated by "mule-skinners" and professional fighters whom barge captains hired to bully their way through the locks in front of other boats. Roustabouts who moved freight and deckhands of canal boats added their share. Whitehall was no place for the faint-hearted; its reputation as a wild preserve where an innocent bystander could be clawed did little to allay a traveler's suspicion that he was taking his life in his hands merely by transferring to a northbound boat or southbound train.

Hemmed in on the east by a great grey palisade of rock, the town straddled the basin and the three locks rising forty feet to the canal. Every boat passing through them was drawn by a huge horse whose legendary strength, even with the springhalt, was equal to a team of three or four mules towing single file. As soon as the mules delivered the boat to the horse at the entrance to the locks, they were stabled on the main street in a long row of sheds, soon to return to the next line station twelve miles to the south, whence a fresh team had already departed with their burden. After a few hours' rest the first team would draw another northbound boat back to Whitehall.

Even dingier than the sheds (which also served the mules as a shelter during the winter when the canal was frozen) were the shan-

ties of the wild breed that drove
them. The fearful reputation they
gave Whitehall was borne out by
our trip down the main street.
While peering into a rookery as
we wandered in a breeze laden
with the aroma of mule sheds and
damp lock timbers, Barney collided
with a man straggling along from
the other direction.

"Hey, punk!" he said, cuffing
Barney across the cheek. "Pull in
your neck!"

"Sorry," said Barney. Unshaven
and unshorn with a scar on his
cheek, the man looked formidable.

"Wanna fight?"

"What for?"

"Blockin' the channel, punk!"

"He ain't done nothin'," said
one of his cronies. "Let's move on."
They might have done so had Barney's husky forearm not caught
their eye.

"You do arm twistin', kid?"

Barney looked alarmed as he
fumbled for an answer. "Not
much." With that his antagonist
was down on his stomach flexing
his right arm, and his friends were
placing bets and digging in their
pockets for coins. With escape out

of the question, Barney had no alternative but to drop down, prop up his arm, spread his legs, and seize the man's hand. The first bout was a stand-off, but his opponent was full of rum and on the next two tries, with the broad palm that had shoveled several thousand tons of coal, Barney made short work of him.

The man who bet on Barney laughed hoarsely and held out his hand to receive the others' coins. "That oughta learn ya, Rupe!" Dumbfounded to have been beaten so easily, Rupe shuffled to his feet as Barney scrambled to his, brushing himself off. We lost little time leaving the scene, walking rapidly without seeming to, and glancing over our shoulders to make sure they weren't taking after us.

"Just my luck to run into a slooney like that," said Barney as we made a bee-line for the *Gloria*. "We could have had the whole bunch on us!" After hearing our adventure, the Chief presumed we'd found the mischief we were looking for and had had excitement enough for one day. We'd been up since dawn, and while the Chief finished his cigar in the dim light of the pilot house, we bedded down on the bunks along the side of the cabin.

CHAPTER

To New York via the Canal and the Hudson! We Embark on a Palace

THE CHIEF WAS WRONG IN HIS PRE-diction of fair weather. As we entered the first lock early the next morning, water was pouring in as relentlessly from above as below. To rise twelve feet in such a deluge seemed like magic. One cannot appreciate a lock's mechanism until the gates close behind him and those in front presently open as he floats into a higher world.

The Chief asked if we knew we'd lost elevation and gained it at the same time. There was a catch in this, as in much else he said. To pass under the canal's low bridges, sailboats had to step their masts, as did small steam vessels their funnels. The *Gloria*'s had been designed with hinges that permitted us to lower it with block and tackle. In doing so we had obviously decreased her elevation!

The roar of water from the canal tumbling into the rocky basin soon faded away and we found ourselves

67

on a peaceful creek aimlessly wandering among steep ledges and verdant hills. The cows in their misty pastures, the rows of cornstalks in the fields, and the dripping woods cast a spell. We were not accustomed to willows brushing the pilot house, leaves fluttering to the deck, or pigs and geese so close we could touch them with our pike poles. Every so often mules appeared along the bank with their preposterous burdens in tow. When two of these passed abreast it was often possible to cross the canal by jumping from one to the other. The bargemen's families lived in odd-shaped cabins opening on to awning-covered back porches where laundry flapped over the stern. Though the cargo was their children's only playground, I thought them fortunate indeed to have seen more of the world from their moving front yards than had Barney and I—the world of the canal and the Hudson from Troy to the sea.

So that the wash from our propeller would not erode the banks, our speed between the locks was limited to five knots. No tug with-out a special permit could navigate the canal, nor any barge drawing more than four and a half feet, since the depth of the water scarcely exceeded that. Though sailing vessels might raise their masts after passing under the bridges, they were still at the mercy of the wrong wind, or none at all. Thus mules prevailed on the hard-trodden towpaths. Near the bank we saw a competitor of the days before the railroad: the hulk of an old passenger barge that still revealed the cabins where travelers slept while teams of horses in relays hauled them the sixty-six miles from Troy to Whitehall.

The shape of this country was as different as its traditions, and we had almost passed Fort Edward before I thought of Jane McCrea, whom Parson Bugbee never mentioned in his lectures because she lived south of the lake, but whose fate Mr. Lampwood had discussed with us in school the previous winter. She was engaged to a young British officer with General Burgoyne's army that sailed from Canada in 1777 and disembarked at Skenesboro, as Whitehall was then called. But the reunion near Fort Edward where Jane awaited her lover never took place. She was taken captive by the Iroquois who killed her in an argument among themselves. Later they appeared at headquarters with her blond scalp. General Burgoyne would have executed the murderer, one of his own troops, had the Iroquois not warned him that if he did so they would all desert his army. The guilty Indian was pardoned instead and the name of Jane McCrea echoing through the woodlands spelled the defeat of ten thousand Redcoats. A tangle of trees felled by local axemen and swarms of giant mosquitoes in the swamp now traversed by the canal delayed them nearly a month. Shortly thereafter, outside the town for which the *Bennington* was named, a detachment of this ponderous cavalcade fell victim to the White and Green Mountain militia, foreshadowing the later eclipse of Burgoyne's whole army at Saratoga.

The motley crews and cargoes fascinated us as they lined up at the twenty locks, all opened and closed by hand. The bridges, too, claimed special attention, for we had to lower the funnel for nearly every one. We failed to count them but there must have been nearly a hundred and fifty, some of iron, some of iron and wood, and some entirely of wood roofed over. Most, however, were humble open ramps with tranquil processions of cows crossing from pasture to pasture each morning and evening.

We spent two days on the northern canal. On the third, early in the morning near Waterford, we met puffing tugs and deep-laden barges just off the Erie Canal from Syracuse, Rome, Utica, Herkimer, Little Falls, Amsterdam, and other fabled places toward the Great Lakes. Barney thought we ought to forget the *Bennington*, the *Republic*, and Cap'n Bullard and follow this silver ribbon westward into another life; but the Chief said a Yankee could no more swap Champlain for Erie water than a catfish could shed its whiskers.

Our excitement quickened as we descended the deepening Hudson. Three cups apiece of the *Gloria's* blackest coffee and the swells of a line steamer half again as long as the *Republic* opened our eyes so wide the Chief was worried they'd leave their sockets by the time we got to New York. Ruffled by a faint breeze from the south, the grey river turned blue and the rain-washed shores glistened in the sunrise.

Our stop for coal among all the ships and boats at the great smoking port of Albany was brief because the Chief was anxious to keep going; the sooner we got to Hoboken, the sooner they could measure the old filler piece against the new one being cast. Yet the sooner our arrival, the easier it would be for Barney and me to catch the returning night boat as we had promised. If we reached New York after six we would be too late and of course have no alternative but wait until tomorrow. This pleasant possibility we discussed in whispers.

Five minutes after leaving Albany, the *Gloria*'s little engine began to relax with falling steam pressure.

"What's the matter?" asked the Chief. "Too much excitement?"

"Nope," said Barney. "The shovel's too heavy."

"And I just got this awful crick in my back," I complained.

"Well then, supposin' you open the boiler door and set down and make a game of who can hit the fire with the most coal."

"We can try, but my arm feels heavier'n lead."

"And my crick goes right into my finger tips."

We opened the door to the boiler, sat down, and each picked up a lump of coal. Barney held his up and turned it around, inspecting it from every angle. "Nice shape to this piece of coal," he said.

"No two of 'em alike," I agreed.

Barney threw his at the boiler but it hit the edge of the door and dropped back. "That was a rotten shot. Now you try." Mine was so wide of the mark it missed the door by a foot. The steam pressure, down several pounds, was falling steadily.

"What's come over you two?" asked the Chief, looking back from his perch on the pilot house stool. "Ten minutes ago you was busier'n a cow's tail in fly time."

"Too much to take in, I guess," said Barney, throwing another hunk of coal at the boiler. This one glanced off the door and into the fire. "Oops!" he laughed, "that was a mistake." We started giggling as more bad shots rained against the side of the furnace. "We've been pushin' the engine pretty hard, Father. What difference does it make if we get to New York at five or seven?"

"Now I see!" nodded the Chief. "You got me over a barrel. S'posin' you was to hear we got a tide to buck in the North River and couldn't make New York by six if we burned pitch pine?"

"Funny thing," said Barney. "My arm don't feel as heavy as it did. How about your crick?"

"It comes and goes. I think it's going!"

The fire quickly revived and as the pressure rose the cranks resumed their lively pace. The sun having dispelled the fog that clung to the eastern bank, and warmed the breeze, we spent much of the morning on deck watching the pageant of sail and steam on the deepening river. Though I had never been north or south of Lake Champlain, I had often sailed the Hudson in my dreams, and excitedly identified the mouth of the Katz-Kill which tumbled out of the craggy Katzburgs where Rip Van Winkle slept, and the ghostly crew played at nine-pins. Fact and fancy were all jumbled together. Aboard the high-pooped *Half Moon* Henry Hudson was searching for the Northwest Passage, and Captain Kidd was rowing ashore to bury his strong box. Robert Fulton's *Steam Boat* was weighing anchor at Clermont on her way to Albany. Athens, Hudson, Saugerties, Kingston: I had heard of them all between blows at the forge during the long winters at the shipyard.

Square foot for square foot the little port of Rondout was the busiest on the river, for it was the outlet of the Delaware and Hudson Canal that led from the mountains of Pennsylvania. Since no berth was available, we tied the *Gloria* to a canal boat and stumbled over piles of flagstone as we carried coal from the dock. As at Albany, we protested shoving off so quickly; we wanted to explore every inch of waterfront and inspect all the boats. The Chief assured us that their vertical beam engines were all like ours, and that New York was the place to keep our eyes peeled. Manhattan had 360 degrees of shoreline. There'd be clippers and other windjammers along South Street and blocks of wharves thick with steamships and steamboats. The definitions of a ship and a boat now being called for, the Chief observed that while ships were supposed to belong to salt water and boats to fresh, steamboats longer than most ships were abundant on Long Island Sound, which was "saltier than the pork that came out of Aunt Agatha's brine."

Our excitement in the evening as the *Gloria* entered the incoming tide in the lower river beneath the lofty Palisades was beyond reckoning. Nothing in our experience compared with a panorama so wondrously new. Barney, who enjoyed posing as an experienced, if not indifferent, man of the world, looked like a little boy, his brown eyes wide with awe as the great *Drew* of the People's Evening Line swept past on her way to Albany, her white bulwarks as long as a city block, her twin funnels high as factory smokestacks. She was gone almost as soon as she appeared, the windows in her turtle deck glimmering in the twilight, her immense wheels laying white water on the darkening river. Were it not for her mountainous swells rolling shoreward, almost tipping our coffee pot off the cylinder head, it would have been easy to dismiss her as a huge jeweled phantom in an outlandish dream.

The sky was dark when we reached New York, but the shores were aglow and the river's shadowy shapes flickered far and near like fireflies. Neither Barney nor I would have steered even if the Chief had asked us to. Familiar water is baffling enough at night without ferries darting from a dozen slips, tows crossing one's bow, and tugs backing and filling in every direction. But the Chief didn't mind.

"We're scared of what we don't know," he said, taking a broad swing north of the Battery before crossing to Hoboken. "My first trip I felt like a pullet in a cockfight. Know your rules, hold your

course, and don't let 'em bluff you." He searched his pockets for a cigar, but they were all gone. "Sightseein's poor at night," he said at length. "The *Gloria*'s tired."

"We aren't," said Barney.

"You wouldn't admit it if you was. When you roll out at sunup you'll look like the last of pea time. I know what you boys are thinkin'. You want me to turn you loose in the city, but the waterfront's no place at night. Shanghaiin' ain't dead. There's still many an old bucket with a crew that was blackjacked."

"How old do I have to be to take care of myself?" asked Barney.

"Seventeen up on the lake and seventeen down here is two differferent things," said the Chief. "You're strong, all right, and smart, but you ain't wise enough. Remember the pickle you got into at Whitehall?"

"That wa'nt our fault. We were mindin' our own business."

"But others ain't. That's just it. Tomorrow you can spread your wings all over New York. Long as you're at the People's Line pier at five-thirty."

Barney and I couldn't fall asleep until after midnight, and our condition at 5 A.M. was accurately prophesied. After calling us twice with no response other than a faint stirring, the Chief emptied the water jug on Barney's face. He rose up sawing the air as if he had gone down for the third time. The Chief, good as his word, suggested we immediately cut loose and take the ferry for New York.

"You got no fish to fry here. Leave your carpet bags with me. I'll bring 'em to the pier at five."

From the moment the creaking double-ender disgorged us at 14th Street in New York until it was time to start for the People's Line pier we could never recall how we got where we went. We must have walked five miles before we climbed on a horse car headed in the wrong direction just so we could sit down. Our objective was the Battery, which we reached by way of the fish market. No spectacle real or imagined could compare with the flotilla of steam and sail on the lower East and North rivers—nor any music with the slushing of their paddles, the chuffing of their ex-

hausts, or the "Yo-heave-ho" at their capstans.

The blackened painting of the square-rigger on the *Bennington*'s donkey-room wall and the clipper model in Captain Hawley's stateroom came startlingly to life, their bowsprits reaching clear over the street, their shabby figureheads and weathered spars confirming the fading age of sail. As if in defiance of steam, a few industrious masters were directing their crews at caulking and painting, which gave the breeze the familiar fragrance of oakum and turpentine. The cool doorways of the ship chandlers facing the piers smelled of manila cordage, and some of the freight piled along the bulkheads was redolent of spices and tobacco.

"Avast there, you swabs! Clear the poop deck!" Barney commanded an imaginary crew. "You in the crow's nest!" he shouted, looking up and cupping his hands to his mouth. "Wake up! This ain't no flop house!" From Captain Grizzlegruff he reverted to Barney Barnaby. "I wouldn't mind shippin' out on one of those."

"Not me," I said. "You could

be gone six months or a year."

"What's the matter with that? Think of all the places you'd go."

"I'd feel lost."

"I'd rather be lost than found," said Barney.

"But sooner or later you'd want to come back," I allowed, "and you have somebody to come back to."

"So do you."

"I mean your parents, your grandfather, and your aunt. All I have are Mrs. Mayberry and Uncle Reuel."

"Don't forget me," said Barney, sensing I was having one of my lonely spells. He put his hand on my shoulder.

"I mean the lake is enough of a world for me," I said. "It's too big here, and all these people. Anyway, I like steam better than sail."

"That's because you know more about steam."

"You don't know anything about sail, either."

"And prob'ly never will," admitted Barney, "because it'll all be gone, the way things are goin'."

"I thought you wanted to be an engineer," I said.

"I do. I'm just kiddin'. Except it must be excitin' to sail way off somewhere."

"Exciting! Who needs more excitement than we've had? First the *Republic*'s pressure went to eighty-three pounds and we got thrown off for fighting. Then we hit the dock at Bluff Point, then the *Bennington*'s filler piece cracked, and now they're building an opposition boat."

"Just the same I get these wanderin' pains," said Barney, "and sometimes they really hurt. Prob'-ly they'll go away. I know there ain't a boat in the world to compare with the *Republic*, or even the *Bennin'ton*."

"Supposing you were an engineer at sea," I said. "You wouldn't get to handle the engine because you'd just be going and going and all you'd see is water every day. There's always something doing on the lake because we land so often."

"I s'pose I'll be married and live on the Point and never leave the lake again."

"Who do you suppose the fair damsel will be?"

"Dunno. She ain't appeared yet.

One thing, no barns for me, emptyin' all those damn cows mornin' and night. Grandfather likes it. But he ain't ever smelled steam and hot cylinder oil."

"I thought he was on one of the old boats."

"Yup. Hall boy one summer. But the equinoctial storm hit and he puked all the way from Basin Harbor to Cumberland Head and that was the end of it."

When we reached the People's Line pier at the foot of Canal Street we could not have walked another foot if our lives had depended on it. It was half an hour until we were due to meet the Chief, and we lay down on an empty wagon where we tried to believe we would soon be boarding the largest vessel in the world, other than the *Great Eastern*. Her name was the *St. John* and she was 420 feet long, longer even than the pier, the most astounding sight of a day filled with wonders. But the senses can absorb just so much; all we had the power to do was gaze at her from our backs and try to count the windows in her lofty turtle deck four stories above the water. We failed

Brian Seaworthy

in this, for there were so many that it proved impossible to keep track of those already counted. We didn't fall asleep but were only half conscious of the hubbub on the pier which, more than an hour before sailing time, already bustled with carriages and drays. The cries of newsboys rose above the roar of steam and the insistent clanging of a bell. Peddlers beset arriving passengers as they tried to thread their way toward the line at the gangplank.

"I'll be jiggered if it ain't the two tourists, all humped up like burnt boots! You two look like you got some mileage on you. New York ain't all beer and skittles, is it?"

Barney was obviously disappointed not to have spied the Chief first so he could pose as an experienced traveler, wise in the ways of the city. "No," he said, jumping from the wagon and dusting himself off. "It's all boats, 'least the part we saw." My legs felt like stumps as I swung them over the edge of the cart.

"See anythin' you liked better'n the *Republic?*"

"Barney thinks he'd like to ship out on a clipper."

"You'd think different after eatin' the wallpaper paste they feed their crews."

"I didn't partic'ly have a clipper in mind. I just thought I'd like to ship out," grinned Barney.

"I want to hear everythin' you seen," said the Chief, handing us our carpet bags, "but that'll wait. If you don't get in line you'll stand as much chance of hirin' a stateroom as a one-legged man in a rump-kickin' contest."

"Is it true," I asked, "that the *St. John* is the biggest thing afloat since the *Great Eastern?*"

"She's a monster. She's got a seventy-six-inch cylinder, a fifteen-foot stroke, and forty-foot wheels. I used to know her engineer but he's not on her now. Wish I could go aboard but they're workin' on the filler piece tonight and I want to get back to Hoboken. Tell your uncle I'll be startin' back tomorrow or the next day and extend to Cap'n Bullard my warmest greetin's."

As the line moved past the ticket window we dug into our jeans for our meager savings to purchase the cheapest stateroom on the boat. We didn't care a fig that it was barely large enough for the double bunk, the washstand and the pitcher, and our disappointment that there was no outboard window was mild compared to the thrill of boarding the queen of the Hudson. Scrambling into our suits we felt like men of the world as we stepped out into the richly carpeted hall.

For once we ignored the engine room, heading instead for the news and tobacco stand where Barney bought and lit a large cigar. It was the first time I had seen him smoke, but such a minor vice seemed fitting for such a major occasion. We had always supposed the stateroom hall of the *Republic* to be the finest afloat, and so it was for its size. Nothing, however, could rival the *St. John's* embellishments in carved mahogany, in plush, and gilt. The lobby of the American Hotel in Burlington would be lost in her grand saloon, a yawning expanse as high as the boat and half as long, with stateroom galleries curving round the sides, like the balconies of an opera house, and huge pillars supporting the dome in the center. The man in the newsstand told us that the grand staircase of carved mahogany inlaid with white holly had cost twenty-five thousand dollars. Though this was hard to believe, its beauty was such as to remind me of the stairs to Heaven, of which I had often dreamed.

Most of the people were decorated as elegantly as the surroundings. In such company plain suits were barely adequate, providing they didn't look so tight as to suggest hand-me-downs. Apparently to dispel any possible suspicion of our country origin, Barney was assuming the airs of a gentleman.

"I say, theah," he commanded in a voice not quite loud enough to be heard by a hall boy. "Fetch me my tea and crumpets!" He made quite a show of his cigar, smoking it little but removing it from his mouth with exaggerated motions. "I do hope James will be on time with the carriage at Albany. Such a nuisance, these public hacks!" With this he removed his cigar with a sweep of his arm so wide that it collided with the bouquet of a girl about to pass us, knocking

some of the flowers out of her hand.

"Oh!" said Barney, scrambling to pick up the roses on the carpet. "I'm sorry!"

The girl's eyes were smiling. "That's all right. Accidents will happen."

"They always seem to happen to me!" complained Barney, his face quite flushed.

The girl had a small dimple in her chin and when she smiled two others appeared in her cheeks. Though she could not have been older than Barney or younger than I, she looked much more at home in her long satin skirt and organdy waist than I felt in my suit. In her dark hair she wore a peach-colored ribbon exactly matching the color of her cheeks. I had never seen a prettier girl.

Breaking an awkward silence during which we didn't know whether to move on or stay, she asked, "What other accidents have you had?"

"Oh," said Barney, regaining his composure, "nothin' important —just bumpin' into things. This is sure a nice boat, isn't it?"

"Yes, I love it."

"Do you travel much?"

"Yes, quite a lot. Do you?"

"Oh yes," said Barney. "We've been in New York on business."

"What business are you in?"

"Transportation. Steamboats."

"Oh, how interesting! Boats like this?"

"Yes, on Lake Champlain." The *St. John*'s whistle blew. Ordinarily wild horses could not have dragged us from the engine room while getting under way, but this was an extraordinary circumstance.

"I've always heard Lake Champlain is so beautiful. Do you have many boats?"

"Three," said Barney (I presumed he was counting the *Gloria*). "We're in the engine department."

"Gracious, you look so young to be engineers!"

"We started young," Barney explained, holding to his dangerous course. Responding to further questions, he went on at length about the awesome responsibilities of an engineer and the perils of the pilot house. The *Republic* and *Bennington*, as he talked, grew longer, more luxurious, and more difficult to handle by the minute.

"Do you live in New York?" I inquired at last.

"Part of the time," said the girl. "But mostly on the *St. John*."

"On the *St. John*!" said Barney. "How does that happen?"

"My father is the Captain." The deepest blush imaginable started over Barney's collar and rose to the roots of his hair. "And I think," she continued, "he'd enjoy visiting with you. Would you like to go up to the pilot house?"

"Would we!" I replied. "I'll say we would!" The springing of the trap he had set for himself left Barney at a complete loss for words. While we climbed the stairs and passed through the stateroom hall with its succession of paneled doors, he appeared to be reassessing what he had told the girl compared to what he might now tell the Captain. The girl never hinted that she knew as much about steamboats as we, which was probable, and seemed delighted that on one of her hundreds of trips to Albany she had met two boys with whom she had something in common.

Even the lofty lookout I had built into the tree on the Point was

Brian Seaworthy

not as high above the water as the pilot house of the *St. John*. We entered to the creaking of her huge steering wheel as the quartermasters swung her into her course upstream. Through curved windows of glistening plate glass the pilot was surveying one hundred and eighty degrees of river, of New York and New Jersey. The Captain and another man were seated in two ornate chairs under the clock and barometer. The pilot house was no less resplendent with brass than the grand saloon was with gold leaf.

"Father," said the girl, "these boys run steamboats up on Lake Champlain. I thought they'd enjoy coming up here and meeting you. This is . . . I'm sorry, I don't know your names."

"I'm Brian Seaworthy. And this is Barney Barnaby."

"Very glad to see you . . . Lake Champlain . . . did you say Seaworthy?"

"Yes, sir."

"You wouldn't be kin to Jacob Seaworthy, would you?"

"Yes, sir, he was my father."

The Captain shook his head as he took hold of both my hands. "Would you believe it! I knew him well! I suppose you know he was responsible for the design of several boats here. We all had great respect for him." I managed to smile, though momentarily the victim of one of my lonely spells. Immediately sensing this, the Captain changed his tack; he said he'd never seen the *Republic* but was aware of her reputation as the finest of her class.

"We think the *St. John* is pretty fine," I said.

"So she is. But the *Republic* has some features the *St. John* hasn't, such as boilers in the hold. That's the coming thing. How fast does she turn up? Close to twenty knots, doesn't she?"

"Yes, sir," said Barney, finding his tongue. "My father's Chief on her and he once clocked her at exactly twenty."

"There aren't many faster," observed the Captain, "unless they're running the tide." He turned to his daughter. "This is quite a coincidence, isn't it, Jeanie?" He now introduced us to his friend, a Mr. Burnside, and to the pilot and quartermasters, who proved equal to all of our questions. Did they often run on compass course? Did they have trouble figuring the wind and the tide? Had their bell system always been the same? It wasn't like ours. How the minutes raced! We stayed the better part of an hour, fascinated with a vantage point which dwarfed everything else on the river.

Presently the Captain looked at his watch. "Well, boys, I have to go below, but Jeanie and I would like you to join us for dinner at eight-fifteen. Is that too late?"

"Oh no, that would be fine."

"By the way," said the Captain, "what stateroom do you have?" He rang the bell for the purser, who shortly appeared. "Is the Presidential suite occupied?"

"No, sir."

"Good. I want these boys moved into it. My compliments."

"Very well, sir."

Jeanie's smile would have warmed the coldest heart on the river. "You have a surprise coming," she said. "That's the nicest room on the boat." This was so startling a development we could think of nothing appropriate to say as we descended to the hall, where Jeanie and her father left us in care of the purser. Insisting that a hall boy fetch our carpet bags, he unlocked the door to the Presidential suite with his pass key, ushered us in, expressed the hope that we would be comfortable, and left.

"Holio Rolio!" exclaimed Barney.

"It's true," I said. "It must be!" The chairs were of gold, the curtains, the carpet, the picture frames, the leather on top of the desk, even the waste baskets. Three people could have slept comfortably on each of the ornate brass beds draped with gold plush. Imposing as all this was, no occupant of the Presidential suite could have failed to be even more impressed by the adjoining bathroom. It had a six-foot tub supported by iron lion's paws, and towels the size of rugs warmed on polished brass racks piped with steam. Having tried out all the chairs and bounced on the beds, laughing uproariously at our good fortune, we flipped a coin to determine who should have the first bath. Barney, winning the

toss, had no sooner stepped into the tub than there was a knock on the door, which I opened.

"You rang, sir?"

"No, I didn't ring."

The valet—that's what he appeared to be—looked puzzled. "Beg your pardon, sir." He left, but in a few moments was back. "Sorry, sir, but someone here has rung."

"It's only my friend and me, and he's taking a bath."

"Then it is your friend who has rung." Crossing to the bathroom door, he knocked, went directly in, and stood stiffly in front of the bathtub. "You rang, sir?"

"Rang! Rang what?" Barney's face was a study in bewilderment.

"The board shows someone rang."

"No, I didn't ring."

"Beg pardon, sir, you have hung your coat on the bell-pull. Kindly excuse the intrusion, sir." He backed out the door, bowing. Removing Barney's coat from the bell-pull he had mistaken for a hook, I had another fit of laughter as did Barney on recovering from his embarrassment.

Of all the day's events the dinner was perhaps the most memorable. Sandwiches were all we had had since morning, and when we sat down to the Captain's table, decorated with fresh flowers and glistening with sparkling glass and silver, our problem was how to eat everything we could lay our hands on without appearing greedy. But an impasse presented itself, the Captain's special menu:

POTAGE DE VOLAILLE
HORS-D'OEUVRE
POISSONS GRILLÉS
À LA MARSEILLAISE
TOURNEDOS DE BOEUF
MAÎTRE D'HÔTEL
POMMES DAUPHINE
QUARTIERS D'ARTICHAUTS
ÉTUVÉS AU BEURRE
SALADE DE SAISON
BAVAROIS AUX FRAISES
PATISSERIE
CAFÉ

I could understand scarcely a word of it, and Barney's expression, while pondering such choices as "grilled poison," was one of utter consternation. It was only by observing what the others did with their finger bowls that I followed suit and removed mine to the left.

Brian Seaworthy

His menu so preoccupied Barney that when the waiter removed his service plate he had first to set aside his finger bowl. This went unnoticed, but the menu was a dilemma of larger proportions.

"What would you boys like to have?" asked the Captain. In a rare moment of resourcefulness, I said, "It's hard to decide." The pressure was off, for the Captain then turned to his wife, to Jeanie, and to Mr. Burnside, who made their choices in English, which allowed me to say: "I think I'll have that too," and Barney to follow up with: "I'll have the same."

Fortunately the several glasses filled with water and wine took care of themselves, and the problem of which forks and spoons to use at what time was solved by observation. It was the most elaborate dinner I had ever sat down to; Delmonico's could not have catered with greater style. Actually there was little to distinguish the dining room of the *St. John* from that of a large hotel on shore.

Barney was having a gay time with Jeanie but was now far more reserved about his boating experiences, for she had had a few herself, as I had surmised. Listening attentively to our trials in the boiler room, Mr. Burnside, who proved to be the agent supplying coal to the People's Evening Line, confirmed what I already knew: that there was no substitute for the best coal for the simple reason that all of it burned, producing more heat and therefore greater economy. He expected to go to Lake Champlain within a few months and I invited him to call at the Point.

After dinner we toured the engine and boiler rooms, then sat with Jeanie in the grand saloon until after eleven. Scarcely able to keep our eyes open when we returned to our suite, we moved the gold chairs to the windows and watched the river for nearly an hour as we recalled our experiences. All that we had seen and done might well have been a dream. Even Jeanie appeared as a kind of Cinderella, though of course our roles were reversed: it was we, tomorrow, who would exchange this world of fantasy for the northern lake in the lap of mountains that also encircled our lives.

CHAPTER

Wherein the Opposition

Launches the Defiance

And Ice Surrounds Us

THE REAL WORLD LAY ONLY AS FAR away as the train from Albany. Our coach was coupled directly to the locomotive and we rode all the way to Whitehall in a whirlwind of soot. The train, however, was less of an anticlimax than the *Republic*. Since Captain Bullard had gradually replaced her crew with deckhands and waiters to his liking, Gussie and Chief DuFour were our only remaining friends. My hope that by arriving early at the crew's table we could avoid the tyrant of the boiler room and fo'c'sle was blighted.

"Well, if it ain't the prize fireman an' his dock-bustin' friend! It's back to the nursery for you, eh, Junior? Between Junior an' Barney an' his ol' man the *Bennin'ton*'ll be at the bottom of the lake yet!"

Gussie's nose was twitching. "If your mouth was any bigger, your head would be an island! Shut your lousy mouth!" But Jib didn't. He

89

Brian Seaworthy

began to recite our mishaps to the new members of the crew. Presently Barney caught my eye, tossed his head in the direction of the door and we got up and left.

"Some day—and it ain't far off —I'm gonna really crack his skull! Fat chance on this boat!" We decided to pay for our supper but had not long been seated in the dining room when Captain Bullard, trundling toward his table, grunted that the kitchen was the place for us and that the dining room was for paying customers. I said we were not members of the crew and had every intention of paying, which elicited merely a "Humph." We did not run into him again, for we spent the rest of the trip with Chief DuFour in the donkey room describing the wonders of New York and the *St. John*. He'd never been farther in any direction than Montreal, where he was born, and while interested in everything we said, had no intention of leaving the lake, for he was timid and mild and did not care for strange places and situations.

"For you," he said, "it is good. For me I t'ink I stay right here."

He seemed rather worn and unhappy, as anyone would whose timidity would not permit him the luxury of standing up to the Captain. But the Chief ruled his engine, and that was enough for him.

Mrs. Mayberry had, by contrast, every intention of getting to New York some day. Her eyes sparkled at our description of the Presidential suite and the *St. John's* richly attired passengers who disembarked at Albany, bound for Saratoga with their retinues, some with grooms and horses with braided tails and bright-colored fly nets. She wondered if the Captain's dinner wasn't an exaggeration; she had always thought finger bowls came after dessert.

Uncle Reuel was in no mood to hear of our experiences. Whatever the risk, there would surely have been less delay in sending the *Bennington's* filler piece by rail. It would take another week to put her back in operation and in the meantime the crew was eating up the profits. There was no recovering the business lost and wages paid while she was laid up. The opposition boat would be launched in

November; her engines and boilers had already arrived at Whitehall where she would be towed for fitting out during the winter. If measured by Uncle's long face, prospects had never been so dreary. I couldn't imagine things being that bad, but of course what I did not understand about the financial affairs of the Company would have filled a bunker. As it happened, the Chief arrived with the new filler piece in three days and in two more, by working from dawn to dark, he put the *Bennington* back in operation.

Shortly thereafter one of her firemen was taken sick and Barney returned to her boiler room while I, unfortunately, returned to school. If I had had a choice it would have been another year with Mr. Lampwood, but he said he had done all he could for me and that he should really have sent me across the bay to the academy the previous fall. Although the shipyard was only three miles as the crow flies from the city waterfront, the *Gloria*'s infrequent trips afforded the only means of getting there. I could and did occasionally take the train, but

there remained a four-and-a-half mile hike over the dirt road from the Shelburne station.

My keep in town was paid by the fund Father had left to support me through college. The food in the modest boarding house near the school was second rate, my room was small and lonely, and my studies none too interesting. Every time the deep whistles of the *Republic* and *Bennington* floated up over the rooftops, I somehow felt bereft of home and country. Whenever I was invited for dinner by classmates, or a friend of Father's who had made a fortune in the lumber business and lived in a splendid mansion on the hill, I was looked upon as an object of pity.

I am perhaps exaggerating my plight. On Sunday excursions I was permitted, despite Captain Bullard's edict, to handle the *Bennington*'s engine, with the Chief on the other bar, of course. On two Saturdays, ordinarily Barney's day off, we made special trips to the way landings in the northern islands to take aboard the apple crop, which often ran to twenty thousand barrels and constituted our heaviest and most pungent loads. So packed with barrels were the gangways back to the paddleshaft, that it was hard to squeeze through.

On October Saturdays we hunted on the Point or fished the nearby reefs. Out of the cold and misty nights the maples brought forth a wonderland of wine, scarlet, and gold, so bright in the morning sun as to shock the senses. Only the lowing of cattle invaded the stillness, and the distant honking of geese flying south over the painted mountains. The stuffy schoolroom in the city and my humdrum boarding house might just as well have been a thousand miles from the vivid out-of-doors at the Point where the realities of land and water seemed to me perfectly blended. Other than a desert, mountain, and river, the long peninsula contained every form of landscape nature could devise. Cut off from the mainland and set adrift it would have vied with the ark as a refuge for the animal kingdom. The domestic creatures of the farms crowding the outbuildings of the shipyard— the dogs, cats, goats, horses, mules, oxen, sheep, pigs, chickens, tur-

keys, ducks, and geese—had their counterparts in the deer, bobcats, raccoons, hedgehogs, fishers, foxes, muskrats, beavers, and jackrabbits that foraged in the hills and lowlands. The seasonal migrations by air brought the hummingbird, the bald eagle, and all the middle-sized birds in between. Such, with its sparkling mountain vistas east across the bay and west over the broad lake, was the Eden we roamed in the fall, sampling as we went its harvest of grapes and apples, all more or less ours for the taking. With a .22 rifle on our last hunting trip we bagged a fox whose skin brought twenty-five dollars at the fur store in the city— exactly one half the reward, with keep, for a month's labor at the shipyard.

Grey November brought the launching of the new steamer at Mark's Bay, an ominous event for which I skipped school. There were not many witnesses afloat, but the hundreds who came from the city in carriages covered the east shore and the new dock west of the ways. The engines and boilers had not been installed, so the superstructure had not been added, yet the hull alone dwarfed the nearby shops and sheds. The Stars and Stripes fluttered at the stern, the Dominion colors amidships, and a blue flag with white stars at the bow, above the dignitaries on the staging.

During the ceremonies a long life was predicted for the new boat, one of her backers declaring that her performance and accommodations would "give the old Company something to think about." The cedar poles supporting the guards every few feet having been knocked away, she was kept upright by keel wedges on the slide ways, which in turn rested on ground ways. Two large chains tightly wrapped around the slide ways fore and aft were all that held her, and as the wife of the New York builder broke a bottle of champagne on her bow, christening her the *Defiance*, four workmen with sledgehammers simultaneously drove the iron pins out of the links binding the chains. With a screech and a groan she started to move, stopped for a moment, which was not considered a good omen, then started again, sliding smooth-

ly into the water to the applause of the crowd. To keep her from the rocks on the small bay's east shore, two tugs diverted her momentum to the west and immediately took her in tow for Whitehall.

One Friday evening in December, shortly after my sixteenth birthday, the creaking of the narrow stairs to my room in town, and a knock on the door, produced to my surprise (I had thought his promise to visit me merely a pleasantry) the urbane and greying Mr. Burnside. Although his interest in selling coal had been apparent during our brief visits in the pilot house of the *St. John* and later at dinner, I had the feeling then and now that he was a kindred spirit. He'd arrived this morning on the *Republic* and had learned my address from Chief DuFour, with whom he had had a long visit.

"The *Republic* is certainly everything you said, and more!" he declared. "But the boiler room—oh my! The Company is losing money there." Economy seemed less important than moral support for Barney, his father, myself, and even the cautious Chief DuFour, in our crusade for manageable coal. Mr. Burnside had not talked with Captain Bullard, who, I pointed out, was in charge of everything. Confessing that he and I were not on the best of terms, and confiding the reasons therefor, I suggested that we see him tomorrow, and if this proved unsatisfactory, which no doubt it would, that we talk with Uncle Reuel.

"If there weren't a clash of personalities," Mr. Burnside observed, "you wouldn't have a steamboat company."

"Before Father died everything was fine here."

Mr. Burnside looked out my window at the gas lamps marking the steep descent of the street to the lake. "The qualities of good skippers tend to filter through the ranks." The conversation now turned to the *St. John*, Mr. Burnside reporting that Jeanie, whom he had seen recently and told of his impending trip to Lake Champlain, had sent us her best wishes. He was spending the night in the hotel, and as I saw him to his rented sleigh he promised to meet me at the pier the next day.

When the *Republic* arrived in the morning, Captain Bullard was standing on the cross deck looking fatter and more imperious than ever. As soon as the gangplank went ashore we stepped aboard and I introduced Mr. Burnside. After a perfunctory handshake, the Captain purposely paid more attention to the departing passengers than to what Mr. Burnside was saying.

"I represent one of the largest companies in the East, furnishing coal to the People's Evening Line, among others. I should like the opportunity to discuss your needs with you."

"There's nothing to discuss," said the Captain. "Our needs are well taken care of."

"I'm confident," replied Mr. Burnside, "that I can meet the price you are paying, or improve on it. If I may say so, after observing the fires on the way from Whitehall yesterday, I am certain I can supply better coal."

"Even if you were not the first salesman who has ever presumed to criticize the operation of the boiler room of this boat, I wouldn't do business with anyone but our present suppliers. We do not deal with every Tom, Dick, and Harry who happens along."

"Are you implying that I am not reputable, or not what I represent myself to be?"

"I'm not implying anything!" snapped the Captain. "I have told you I am not interested."

"I should think you would at least . . ."

"It's a matter of supreme indifference to me what you think!" interrupted the Captain. "You and your friend may step ashore."

"See what I mean?" I asked as we walked toward the sleigh.

"You do have a problem, all right. A big fat one. And the irony of it is that you own the company."

"Yes, but Uncle Reuel is running it, and Captain Bullard doesn't think I even exist." Although I feared our long drive to the Harbor to see Uncle Reuel would also prove futile, Mr. Burnside was indignant enough, and sufficiently interested in my welfare, to want to go whether or not he sold a pound of coal.

Uncle, to my surprise, was in

quite a pleasant frame of mind (I did not learn until a week later that Mrs. Mayberry had agreed to marry him sometime the following year). He welcomed Mr. Burnside with a smile and offered him a brandy as we sat down in the parlor.

"Brian has told me of his experiences on the *St. John* and of the kindness of the Captain and yourself. I have traveled on the Narragansett boats but not on the People's Line."

"Of all the boats I've ridden on," Mr. Burnside declared, "none has a wake smoother than the *Republic*'s. Everything about her seems just right."

"It's the *Bennington* that's giving us trouble," Uncle said.

"From what I could see of her at a distance yesterday, I judged her to be in good shape with many years of service left."

"She's going on fourteen," I volunteered.

"She's due to be hauled out," said Uncle. "Some planks need replacing. I gather from what Brian said you are in the coal business."

"I am."

Brian Seaworthy

"You'd no doubt like the opportunity of selling us some."

"If I can produce better coal at a lower price, yes. I have to say, frankly, that almost any coal would be better than what the *Republic* is burning. You of course know that good coal makes all the difference in handling, economy, clean boilers, and the rest."

Uncle nodded, peering at me over his glasses. "We have had some complaints about the coal."

"I'd be glad to quote you some prices and forward a bargeload for you to try."

"Under ordinary circumstances I would consider it. But our circumstances are not ordinary. I don't know how much Brian has told you. After his father died I came here to help. I then knew nothing about the operation of steamboats. I know more now, and in the future may supervise every aspect of the business. Meanwhile I am relying on the judgment of Captain Bullard whom I have appointed marine supervisor. Before coming here he had long experience on the Great Lakes. He's clever at making economies. The

97

figures on his boats speak for themselves."

"He's a pretty hard man to talk to," Mr. Burnside said.

"I agree," said Uncle. "But that's the situation." That ended it. The rest of the conversation was amiable enough, but had nothing to do with coal. I was sorry to see Mr. Burnside go, for I liked him and was grateful to him.

"Things may change for the better," he said, getting into his sleigh. "Or else they'll get worse. I hope your uncle's confidence in Bullard is justified. For my own satisfaction I'll try to find out what you pay for coal and who your down-country suppliers are. I have a good many connections. If I learn anything, I'll write you." He gave me his card and shook my hand warmly. "If I can help in any way, son, let me know."

Although the broadest parts of the lake did not freeze until later, ice in the Narrows and in the bays drove the boats into the Harbor shortly after New Year's. While they could easily cut through an inch or more, ice formed very fast on quiet zero nights and there was always danger of being caught in Whitehall for the winter. More than once passengers and freight had been landed and taken aboard from stages and teams on the ice at the entrance to the breakwater at Plattsburg, whose shallow harbor froze early. During the last weeks it was often necessary to turn the engine over while tied to the dock in order to break the ice around the wheels and hull. Except for a channel which the *Gloria* had kept open, the bay was frozen solid when the boats came in, and within three days there were as many inches of new ice in the channel.

A few weeks later the ice field extended clear from the Point to the city, completely altering the landscape. Fishing shanties appeared in colonies, and ice-cutting crews started work. A narrow channel led from the place they were harvesting it around the end of the breakwater to the shore. A line of men with pike poles pushed the heavy cakes through the channel until they could be eased onto an endless chain which carried them from the Salt Dock slip through an underground passage up into the

ice house on the other side of the street. As soon as a road over the ice to the Harbor was "bushed," or outlined, with evergreens, I was able to skate, snowshoe, or walk there every Friday afternoon, returning Sunday evening in the *Gloria*'s winter counterpart, the shipyard sleigh, en route to pick up the workmen in town. All the shipyard supplies in winter came by ice. Much traffic also crossed the broad lake on roads carefully bushed to avoid the cracks and ridges that developed from the pressure.

Bound in its straight-jacket, the lake on mild days was as pastoral as any snow-covered plain. In a blizzard or windstorm the trek to the Harbor could be fearful, with steam rising in angry columns from the fissures in the ice, deep drifts obliterating the road, and the driving snow cutting like tiny chips of glass. Even at my back, the wind on such days penetrated my sheepskin coat and heavy woolen shirt and underwear so that the last mile seemed like a hundred. Facing the north on my return to the city, I was most often buried under a buffalo robe in the sleigh.

99

Almost as much went on at the shipyard in winter as aboard the boats at the height of the summer season. As soon as they were safely secured with a network of two-inch lines, their boilers were blown down, washed, and inspected, and their engines laid up before they froze. All the lifeboats were lowered, carried ashore, and turned over on the hill. Every stick of furniture in the staterooms, halls, and dining rooms—chairs, sofas, and heavy marble-topped tables—had to be stored in the various sheds. All the Axminster carpets, every last piece of tableware, and even the gilt eagles on the masts, were removed and stored.

The task of protecting the boats from the pressure of the Bay's large field of ice was unending. No sooner had we cut a six-foot channel outside them than new ice appeared and soon our thin-bladed channel axes were flying again. Two or three inches were purposely allowed to accumulate immediately around the hulls so that work could be done on the oak rubbing guards. Standing on the ice was the only way to reach them, other than from

a staging in drydock. The hull inspector did not judge the condition of the *Bennington*'s planks to be serious, so her hauling was postponed until the following winter.

On the coldest days only the wood smoke billowing from the stack of Old Bess, the shop boiler, and the panting of the exhaust from the stationary engine she fed with steam, testified that the snow-covered shipyard was alive. Without Old Bess there could be no heat, no sawmill, no machine, carpenter or blacksmith shop, a fact that "Ashes" Robarge, who had tended her for nearly three decades, wouldn't allow anyone to forget. Through him she acquired a personality whose moods ranged from tranquil to tempestuous.

"Bess ain't been so good lately," Ashes would declare, laying the trouble to a falling barometer. Or, "Bess is sure feelin' her oats this mornin'." Those who knew Ashes soon learned that the supply of hard cider he kept at hand, and the amount of it in him at any given time, had more to do with Bess's condition than her age or temperament, for he would put off cleaning her tubes until he felt like it. If they were full of soot, naturally she would not steam easily.

As soon as Bess was up to pressure each morning, Ashes would turn the throttle valve on the big upright engine as solemnly as if he were setting the world in motion. Then he threw the lever engaging the wandering shafts, wheels, and slapping belts harnessed to the machinery upstairs, which in turn answered with a whining and rumbling. Bess's frugal diet consisted of shavings and scraps shoveled through a trap door from the adjoining sawmill, for which she in turn furnished the power. This always seemed to me an approximation of perpetual motion, though the ultimate source of energy was of course the rafts of oak, pine, and spruce towed to the Harbor by the *Gloria*. The heavy logs were hauled up the bank with teams and piled outside the sawmill.

When very young Barney and I found no contrivance more joyful than the ancient up-and-down saw which slowly but inexorably sliced its way through a trunk sixty feet long. The log was chained on a long carriage which advanced inch by inch toward the saw in the shed. As soon as the cut was completed we would jump on the carriage which, at the throwing of a lever, withdrew at a delightful clip to the starting point sixty feet back, ready for another cut. While one log lay on the carriage, a second was being peeled with an adze and brought forward with a snatch block. The lumber was stacked in surrounding sheds where a variety of sizes and lengths was always available to replace hull planks, decking, or side-housing.

The shops appealed to none of the senses so strongly as to that of smell: the burning wood of the boiler room, the steam and hot cylinder oil of the engine room, the sawdust of the carpenter shop, and over it in the loft, the drying stacks of butternut, cherry, mahogany, walnut, and birch; the cutting oil of the machine shop, the turpentine and white lead of the paint shop, the hemp and canvas of the rigging room.

The pace in the shops was deliberate. Careful work, whether straightening guard iron, reboring

Brian Seaworthy

cylinders, or mixing and curing deck paint, took as long as necessary. One of my tasks each Saturday was stirring the yellow-orange paint which had to be mixed several months before it was used. Ten gallons contained thirty-five pounds of yellow ocher, five of red lead, and ten of white, seven of boiled oil, and a half-gallon each of Japan drier and turpentine. No other color or consistency had ever been used on the wooden and canvas decks of our boats or, to my knowledge, any others like them.

The winter days were short of light and long on talk. In the smoking room of the boarding house, its air heavy with tobacco and kerosene, every tidbit of gossip about the opposition boat was snapped up.

"You can bet your store teeth she ain't ever gonna' pass the *Republic*." (Long pause as the men smoked their pipes.)

"Why ain't she?"

"Because we didn't build her." (Another long pause.)

"Her hull sure is slick as a schoolmarm's leg."

"Some schoolmarms with slick legs ain't very fast."

"How would you know? You ain't never been in a schoolroom."

"Schoolmarms ain't always *in* school."

"It ain't only her hull. It's her boilers and en-jine."

"Boilers ain't what they used to be. Now you take the iron in Old Bess . . ."

"Wanna know where the iron is, Ashes? In your head!"

The talk was casual but uneasy; competition had always brought austerity in which no one's job was safe. While it is not in the nature of boys to brood, except briefly, not a day passed without a few moments of gnawing anxiety over what next summer would bring. Since Uncle never discussed finances with me, presumably because it would be time wasted, I found myself one afternoon asking the bookkeeper, Mr. McGettrick, what he thought. His office was only an alcove back of the stairs on the second floor of the shop, but the winter sun through his single window cast a certain cheerfulness on his high desk piled with ledgers.

"What do I think?" he asked, setting down his quill pen and running his hands through the frizzled hair surrounding his bald pate. "Faith, laddie, I wish I knew what to think!" For a few moments he whistled softly through his teeth, which he was always doing whether or not he was pleased. "Your uncle had me turn over the boat ledgers to Captain Bullard last spring, and last summer he took care of the shop payroll as well."

"Why does Captain Bullard have the ledgers?"

"Years ago the captains all did their own accounting. Then your father had all the books brought here."

"Did Captain Hawley take care of the *Bennington's*?"

"I think not," said Mr. McGettrick, hooking his heels over the rungs of his high-legged stool. "Every few days he turned over his receipts to Captain Bullard. The payrolls and accounting for the boats were all taken care of in the purser's office of the *Republic*."

"But the boats aren't running and Captain Bullard is away, so where are all the ledgers now?"

"Your uncle hasn't told me, lad-die, and it's not my business to ask."

"Do you think Captain Bullard is honest?"

"I've no reason to think he isn't."

"And none to think he is?"

Mr. McGettrick shrugged his shoulders in a way that indicated he did not wish to pursue the subject. He took up his pen, dipped it in the inkwell, then put it down.

"Bookkeepers just put figures in books," he said with a fleeting apologetic smile. Then he swiveled around on his stool and looked me straight in the face. "You understand, laddie, that bookkeepers' families have to eat."

CHAPTER

A Sad Race, Piracy at Midnight, Some Grim Revelations and Results

I<small>T WAS ANNOUNCED IN</small> M<small>ARCH</small> that the *Defiance* would be ready to sail from Whitehall as soon as the ice went out. This was hardly news to the marine fraternity. For weeks we had been awash with reports about her engine and the luxury of her staterooms and yet unfinished hall. Her vaunted power was our ultimate worry. If she were even a mile-an-hour faster than the *Republic*, she would win all our business she could carry.

As the winter waned Chief Barnaby, by nature an optimist, confessed to feeling "bluer'n a whetstone," while Captain Hawley went about his tasks almost in silence. Announcing that she didn't know whether she wanted "to go boatin' this year," Gussie finally agreed when she found she could go with Captain Hawley and the Chief on the *Bennington*. Uncle's disposition, curiously enough, was better than at any time since his arrival—perhaps because Captain

Bullard had told him we could now stand any amount of opposition. Or perhaps because Mrs. Mayberry had agreed to a Christmas wedding, to be followed by a voyage to Australia to visit relatives she hadn't seen in years.

Still confined to the Harbor, the *Republic* and *Bennington* awaited the wind that would carry away the ice now rotting under the April sun. Forbidden to go boating until I had finished my examinations in June, I was reduced to praying that the big wind would blow on a Saturday or Sunday. It came with a roar in the darkness early on a Friday, the *Republic* heading for Whitehall at sunup and the *Bennington*, with Barney firing for his father, taking on freight for Plattsburg. Awakened with a start by her booming whistle, I could hardly wait for classes to end, for I had hatched a plan to which Uncle could have no reasonable objection: I would take the train to Rutland and the stage to Whitehall, spend the night on the *Republic*, and ride her back on the first day of her war with the *Defiance*.

I hated the new boat, but as the stage rattled through the shadows late in the evening, I could not wait to see her. My first glimpse, in darkness partly dispelled by the gas lights in her hall and the lanterns on the pier, confirmed my worst fears. Although she had already taken on quantities of freight she looked like a great swan, so very white that except for the *Republic*, tied up a few rods away, everything around her seemed ordinary. Her paddlewheels were decorated with paintings of arches or tunnels revealing landscapes of Adirondack scenery. The port side displayed a gorge with a group of deer, and the starboard a stag with Whiteface Mountain appearing through a trough in the hills. The carved head of a deer adorned her bow. Three of her flagstaffs bore the gilded antlers of moose and elk. At least these, I consoled myself, could not compare with the *Republic*'s carved eagles.

The boats were not scheduled to sail until morning, but already the docks were nothing but confusion. The specter of competition had come to life as suddenly as Grandfather laid it to rest years ago. Reappearing out of thin air a swarm of agents or "runners" were forcing handbills on every bystander and seizing the luggage of prospective passengers as they hollered: "Take the *Defiance*!" "Defy the monopoly."

But this was mere prelude to the scene next morning before sailing time when the train out of Albany emerged from the tunnel beneath the town and canal and screeched to a halt, as runners shouted from the platform: "Lake Station! This way to the fastest boat!" Passengers scarcely knew what was happening as they and their trunks were spirited aboard the new vessel. But the *Republic* was quietly winning her share, for her name was a household word with travelers, whereas most of them had never heard of the *Defiance* and did not know or care where she was going.

A half-hour before sailing time, unrecognized by anyone, I crossed the *Defiance*'s gangplank, paused to view her engine, then climbed the stairs to her stateroom hall. Although the same in length, 160 feet, its woodwork and furnishings were strikingly different from those of the *Republic*. The chestnut doors to the cabins were covered with flowers and figures of deer carved in black walnut, as were the sofas, chairs, and marble-topped tables. Daylight through the turtle deck's opaque glass windows, etched with the coat of arms of New York (the *Republic*'s bore the crest of Vermont), would diffuse a soft light on the arched braces of the ceiling and the rose carpet, very dark now under the chandeliers. The stewardess stood at the open door of the "President's Room" calling attention to the French bedsteads of tulip wood and bird's-eye maple, the frescoed ceilings, and crimson upholstery. This room had not been taken, nor had many of the others. Early in the season, until the piles of accumulated freight at way landings could be disposed of, the boats ran day schedules.

Impressive as travelers would find all this, I determined that our hall of cream and gold was more elegant. Or was this wishful thinking? Undecided whether I had seen enough or too much, I descended to the gangplank and picked my way through the freight on the dock to the *Republic* so that I could help Chief DuFour with his wiping and oiling. Had he not offered to share his stateroom the previous night, no doubt Captain Bullard would have seen to it that I paid for one. I could have slept in the fo'c'sle but Jib was firing and I had no intention of going below.

"You see her en-jine?" the Chief asked as he plied the rocker arms with oil from the long-necked copper can.

"I glanced at it."

"What you t'ink?"

"I couldn't see it was any different than this one."

"You see the b'ilers?"

"No, but they carry fifty-three pounds, same as ours. I saw the gauge in the engine room."

"Somebody tell me her fireboxes a little larger."

"Would that make any difference?"

"Maybe. You see anyt'ing funny about her paddlewheels?" I hadn't.

"They rest low in the water. All the time t'ree, maybe four, bucket in the water. That's not so good, I t'ink."

"Why not?"

"Because if her wheels too low," said the Chief, setting down his oil can so he could explain with his hands, "her buckets carry too much water on the way up, and that slow her down."

"I hope so," I said. The whistle blew. Within a moment the *Defiance* countered with a blast. I went out on the cross deck.

The maiden voyage of the *Great Eastern* itself could not have caused more excitement. Shouts from the rails and from the dock and shore were punctuated by the shrill whistles of tugs. Since the *Republic* lay to the north, we started first, creeping through the channel on a slow bell. There was little evidence of a race until we had taken on all the freight we could carry at Benson's Landing and Larrabee's and had cleared the Narrows south of Crown Point. The *Defiance*, having also stopped at two landings, was still behind but was gradually gaining for two obvious reasons: our steam pressure was only 47 and the Chief hadn't opened the throttle wide.

"Why aren't we keeping steam?"

Brian Seaworthy

I complained. "They're catching up!"

The Chief looked at the gauge. "Jib keep it between 47 and 50."

"But we should have 52!"

"I know, but you know the Cap'n if he hear the safety blow."

"But it doesn't blow at 52!" I protested. "It blows at 53!" The Chief crossed to the railing over the boiler room.

"Hey, Jib. You got more steam? Fifty pounds?"

"I got what I got!" was Jib's impudent reply. The pressure stayed at 47.

"You and Barney—you keep her at 52, eh?" the Chief said with a wistful smile.

"Why don't you open her up?" I pleaded, knowing well enough why not: at full steam, the Captain claimed we burned a third more coal. "There's a race on!" I begged. "They're going to beat us!" Stepping into the engine room, the Chief opened the throttle a little beyond two-thirds. The rocker arms busily responded to the quickening breath of the valves.

This helped, but not enough. Now only a few rods astern, the

Defiance blew to pass us to starboard, for we were crowding the port side of the channel. From the donkey room window I saw we were still slowly falling back, and that to stay ahead or even to keep up we would need everything we had. Within two or three minutes her bow had reached our quarter and was still creeping forward window by window. Presently she was directly abreast, a few rods to starboard, her wheels throwing great gushers of water and foam. I was beside myself. We still had only 47 pounds, and a good three inches to go on the throttle. Yet I could do nothing, and the Chief dared do no more.

The instant she thrust her bow ahead of ours the *Defiance* blew her whistle. Wildly waving their arms, her passengers jumped up and down, cheering at the top of their lungs. So tightly clenched were my fists, my knuckles were white. The Chief, almost as agitated, started for the engine room, hesitated, turned to look out again, then, gesturing with both index fingers, announced: "I show you somet'ing!" Hurrying into the engine room he

seized the throttle and pulled it all the way down. The wheels and engine responded with a powerful surge. This was going to do it! It was we, now, who were gaining and I who was doing a jig in the donkey room.

Then a frightening thing happened. Although both boats were holding their course, the distance between them began to shrink. Within a few moments the *Defiance* had drawn so near that a line could have been heaved aboard her. Nearer, nearer she drew, alarmingly nearer! Then, as suddenly as if she had run out of steam, she dropped rapidly back, back, back, into our wake. Such was my astonishment, all I could do was stare at her retreating bow. As I turned, dumbfounded, to the Chief, my heart nearly stopped beating. Captain Bullard was standing outside the engine room. Opening the half-door, he stepped inside, grabbed the throttle and drew it back a third. Then, pivoting his huge bulk around, he confronted the Chief with a withering glare.

"Apparently my orders don't mean anything to you!" Unable to find his tongue, even to look up, the Chief stared at the deck. A chubby finger pointed to the Chief's license on the bulkhead. "I'll have that torn into a hundred pieces!"

His license embodied all the Chief was or ever would be. He raised his head, incredulously, his eyes wide with alarm. "No! No! I don't never do it again, Cap'n—never! Body and soul, Cap'n!" He crossed himself. Pulling a red pencil from his pocket, the Captain drew a line just under the throttle on the white metal of the linkage, then pointed the pencil at the Chief.

"That's your life-line. If the throttle goes a sixteenth-of-an-inch beyond it, you'll have no ticket on this boat or any other!"

"The throttle stay where she is, I swear, Cap'n! I never do it today, only I see the new boat going to pass us. . ." The Chief's voice trailed off; the Captain had spied me across the gangway in the donkey room.

"I thought as much!" he declared in a voice as contemptuous as his close-set eyes. Crossing to the doorway, which he almost filled,

he seized my arm. "You are behind this! I have had enough of you! You will get off at Burlington and never step foot on this boat again!" He shook my arm. *"Understand?"* My hair was straight up with resentment and fear.

"You can't order me off this boat," I blurted out. "She belongs to me!"

"Oh can't I? I can come pretty near it! Next time you'll be *carried* ashore. You needn't protest to your uncle. It is I who has been, am, and will be, giving orders!" Shaking my arm again, he turned away and trundled into the recess.

"What I tell you!" the Chief said after a horrified silence. Since I was largely responsible for what had happened, there was little I could say. But what had I done that was so wrong? Here we were, our existence at stake, with 47 pounds' steam pressure and two-thirds' throttle. The criminal, if the *Defiance* passed us, would be Bullard. Was it conceivable that the old reprobate wanted us to lose? I hated every last pound of him—the flat nose, the little eyes in the pale face, the huge paunch, the piano legs and small feet encased in shiny black shoes. Even the Chief, to whom submission had become so much a way of life that he dared not take exception to anyone, much less the Captain, looked as though he could chop him up with a meat cleaver.

"You see what I do to the *Defiance?*" he finally asked, with a faint spark in his mild brown eyes. "The water not deep. When I open her up, our wheels take more water and *pull* the *Defiance* toward us." He drew his hands together. "And the Cap'n of the *Defiance*, he get scared and drop back!" Even under such doleful circumstances this seemed a resplendent bit of strategy. If Chief Barnaby knew of it or ever tried it, he never told us, for fear, perhaps, that it was just the perilous kind of maneuver a fledgling engineer would enjoy trying. Certainly it would have been we who dropped back if Bullard had been steering, weak-headed helmsman that he was known to be. No doubt he was now up bullying the pilot, who instead of veering away, had gamely held our course—and probably enjoyed every minute of it.

Submitting, as we had, without a contest, it was just as humiliating that the *Defiance* passed us some distance away as if she had done so close by. The Chief was convinced, however, that the volume of water her low-set wheels were churning up was costing her a mile or two an hour, that she was expending everything she had, and that we would at least be her equal if we were running at full steam and throttle. If! If your aunt had whiskers, as Chief Barnaby would say, she'd be your uncle!

Steaming regally into Burlington harbor, whistle blowing, flags fluttering, passengers cheering, factory whistles answering, spectators waving, the *Defiance* won the day—and, as it turned out, the summer. Arriving twenty minutes later, we must have looked like suspected codfish. Glumly disembarking as they watched the excitement at the next pier, our passengers knew the *Defiance* now, if they hadn't before, as the boat to take next time. And they did take it. The more business she attracted day by day, and the more we lost, the more bitter we became. Yet

112

the *Republic* continued at two-thirds' throttle, Captain Bullard announcing in the newspaper that he had no intention of turning the lake into a raceway.

In June I received a startling letter from Mr. Burnside, saying that in his pursuit of the details of our coal business he had learned that Bullard was personally receiving a commission for every ton we burned! Uncle, when I excitedly reported this news, quickly took the wind out of my sails. "That is true. Without this commission we could not begin to pay Captain Bullard the salary he deserves for shouldering our responsibilities."

In mid-July Bullard ordered the *Bennington* dry-docked over the vehement protests of Captain Hawley and Chief Barnaby who declared she needed hauling out about as much as a walrus needs a moustache. Never in their experience had they known a boat without a small leak, and neither had Father or Grandfather, who they thought must be turning over in their graves. Abandoning all restraint in a hot encounter greatly relished by Barney and me, the

Chief told Bullard that as a ship-wright he "didn't know enough to suck alum and drool." But the hauling took place as scheduled, right in the middle of the season, depriving the Company of nine days of vital revenue, and bringing on a succession of events as desperate as any in the annals of the Barbary Coast.

Hauling out a thousand-ton vessel required the ingenuity of six decades, all the tackle we had, and the horsepower of every man and beast on the Point. Having been exposed to years of frost and ice, the oak slideways running from the water up past the main shops to the blockhouse were more than a little "out of true." Hence the back-breaking delay when the *Bennington*, two-thirds out of water, but not quite far enough to inspect the leak, got stuck on the ways. Seven men driving seven pairs of horses against sweeps attached to seven capstans—fourteen men at seven other capstans taking up slack—the seven enormous lines, stretched tight as fiddle strings a thousand feet to the boat through huge groaning sheaves in the blockhouse, could not budge her another inch. Slathering tallow on the ways, Barney and I sweltered for a week in the sweat of men and horses as one line after another let go with a crack, flying against the blockhouse or tangling in a heap. Wearily unsnarling, splicing, re-rigging, tightening and testing the lines, we would start again, as the foreman hollered at the capstan crews: "Stop two! Five, slow! Easy, seven!"

Finally four battering rams were devised in the form of large timbers hung from the guards on both sides of the boat. Four men standing on each of them swung them out; then, swinging back, bumped them against the ways in unison. These were just enough to overcome the inertia, and she moved. As soon as the lines to the horses were tightened, the process was repeated. Inch by inch we got her up only to find, as the Chief and Captain Hawley had anticipated, every plank as hard and true as the day it was cut. A little "corking" in one seam, which could have waited until next winter, or indefinitely, was all she needed. No

epithet in the Chief's large reservoir could match his indignation.

The next morning, Saturday, Barney and I were up at five-thirty building our fires while the boat was still on the ways so that she would be ready to steam to the city the moment she was launched. With a line to the *Gloria*, churning away in the Harbor, she easily descended the greasy ways and at eight o'clock we tied her up at Burlington, ready to resume our schedule Monday morning. Worn down with anxiety and resentment, Captain Hawley announced that he and the Chief would not wait to be paid. Asking that their envelopes be put in the purser's office safe, he and the Chief took the train for Waterbury to spend the weekend fishing at Lake Mansfield with the Captain's brother.

When Captain Bullard boarded the *Bennington*, following the arrival of the *Republic*, he was not carrying the customary satchel with the monthly pay envelopes.

"There are not enough funds," he announced to the crew gathered on the deck, "to meet the payroll of both boats. It will therefore be necessary for you to wait." To the angry mutterings that followed, Bullard explained that Uncle Reuel was in Plattsburg arranging a loan, and that as soon as this was obtained we would be paid. Among the casualties was Gussie, whose wisps of hair stood away from her forehead almost as if they had been charged with electricity.

"There's money enough!" she shouted. "Only it's goin' into the wrong pocket!"

"What's that supposed to mean?" demanded the Captain.

"You ain't foolin' nobody. You mean to starve all the old hands off this boat! Well, there won't be no starvin' long as I got the keys to the larder. We'll invite our friends and eat up every crumb!"

"You're fired!" snapped the Captain.

"Am I?" Gussie shuffled up to the Captain and leered in his face. "I ain't budgin' an inch! Not for no stuffed dumplin' as you!" She looked so fierce as she stamped into the gangway to her stateroom, slamming the door behind her, that momentarily for once in his life the Captain seemed uncertain as to

how to cope with the situation.

"You needn't expect me tomorrow," boomed the Parson, "or on any future excursions!"

"That's immaterial to me," replied Bullard. "The excursion tomorrow is canceled anyway. As for the future we can function without history lessons." Barney looked like a thundercloud but didn't open his mouth for fear we might again be scuttled. I could easily have spat in the Captain's face. In his hand-to-mouth existence the Parson could not even have afforded old Agatha had the shipyard not kept her in oats, not to mention his sleigh and carriage, which we were always repairing. How I wished he would unhinge his tongue, though of course this did not become men of the cloth. Utterly crestfallen as we started for the shipyard on the *Gloria*, he confessed that there were too many Takers in the world to suit him, and that Givers were too often paid with ingratitude. But his spirits rebounded when Mrs. Mayberry, whom he classified as a Giver, invited him to dinner, insisting as she so often had before, that he stay the night.

Brian Seaworthy

With nothing to do until Monday, Barney and I dug some worms, rowed around to the swamp opposite the shipyard on the west side of the Point, and paddled in among the trees to fish bullheads. Only the croaking of frogs disturbed a stillness as deep as the darkness beyond our flickering lantern. Although we had several bites as we maneuvered about among the tree trunks, we had yet caught nothing when a slight cool breeze from the east carried the sound of muted voices. The shipyard was only a short distance that way and we paid little attention until we distinctly heard the words: "... won't last the summer ... take the *Bennington* ..." and, after a pause, "... round up a crew. ..."

"Did you get that?" I whispered. "That sounded like Jib."

"Not the first one—that was Bullard." The breeze slightly shifted and we could catch no more words, strain our ears as we might. Had our attention not been distracted by a fish which snagged Barney's line on a root, eventually breaking it, we would have gone back at once.

"Do you believe in ghosts, Parson?" I asked when we returned to the house.

"Spirits, yes; ghosts, no."

"Aren't spirits the same as ghosts?"

"Not quite. The spirits of the departed are all around us, but not ghosts, stalking about in shrouds."

"We swear we heard Captain Bullard and Jib when we were in the swamp."

"That's just the way ghost stories get started. I don't know about Jib, but Bullard was indeed here."

"He was?"

"He came to pay the farmers whose teams hauled out the *Bennington*, then went back on the *Gloria*."

"He pays them, he pays the *Republic*'s crew," muttered Barney. "Everybody but us."

"Mark my word!" the Parson predicted in a sepulchral voice. "He'll pay in the lowest, hottest regions of Hades! What did you think you heard?"

"Something like 'won't last the summer' and 'take the *Bennington*.'"

"Perhaps it is his strategy,"

suggested the Parson, "to starve us so *we* won't last the summer!" Sensing that for the moment he had failed as an apostle of hope and strength, he intoned, "We mustn't allow ourselves to become discouraged. Remember that though His ways are often mysterious, the Lord is ever at our side." Presently he arose. "It's time to climb the golden stairs, boys. You going home tonight, Barney?"

"No," replied Mrs. Mayberry, the great provider. "He's staying here. Breakfast at eight so Agatha will have plenty of time to make Hurricane Hill."

"My sermon will be 'Saints in our midst.' And you, my dear, are one of them. You boys will be going with us, I presume?"

"We're conducting our own outdoor service here," replied Barney resourcefully, disarming the Parson with his grin.

The day's events weighed on my mind that night like a millstone —and revolved like one. If, according to Bullard, the Company was in such good condition that we needn't worry about the *Defiance*, why had Uncle Reuel gone to Plattsburg for a loan? Because, I supposed, the *Bennington* hadn't been earning anything lately. And whose fault was that? Bullard's! Uncle must at last be having misgivings about him. High time! Why had Uncle gone to Plattsburg when we had always got all the money we needed in Burlington? Perhaps, I feared, the Burlington bank wouldn't loan us any more.

The moon seemed to have crossed the whole sky, and I was still staring at the ceiling. Listening with mounting annoyance to Barney's measured breathing, I at length got up and looked out the window. The bay was bathed in silver. I could see the outline of the far shore and the hills beyond, but the mountains were lost in a luminous mist. To the northeast the perpendicular cliff of Red Bluff Point was overlaid with light and shadow. Gazing further north, I had the start of my life. In the distance, white as snow in the moonlight, the ghost of the *Bennington* was drifting slowly toward Mark's Bay. I squeezed my eyes tight but when I opened them she was still there. For a few moments I stood

transfixed, trying to convince myself that this was somehow an illusion.

"Barney! Get up! QUICK!" Popping up like a jack-in-the-box, Barney tottered to the window, his face thick with sleep. I pointed to the north.

"My God! It looks like the *Bennington*!" he exclaimed, his eyes staring wide. "It *is* the *Bennington*!" She was moving, ever so slowly, toward the dock outside the ways where the *Defiance* was launched. I rushed to awaken the Parson and Mrs. Mayberry, and brought them to my window.

"Two-thirty!" the Parson exclaimed, looking at his watch. "What in the name of Heaven do you make of it?" We all went down to the kitchen, Barney and I alternately gulping tea and going to the porch to see if she was still there. The Parson's judgment was that daylight would make better sense of whatever was happening. "Wouldn't you know Cap'n Hawley and the Chief would be away— and your uncle! What ever can we do in the dead of night?"

"Row over and find out!" Bar-

ney suggested. "It's only a mile."

"That's it!" I started for the door. "You want to come, Parson?"

"Great Scott! I don't know. Should I? I'd just be dead weight in the boat."

" 'Course not," said Barney. "We may need some ballast!" Realizing that the die was cast, Mrs. Mayberry was wringing her hands.

"Oh dear, this doesn't sound good at all! For mercy's sake do be careful!"

Within a few minutes we were on our way, the oarlocks creaking with each strong stroke, the Parson in the stern and I in the bow with my eyes fixed on the *Bennington*, now at the dock broadside to the setting moon. So eerie did she seem in such surroundings that we did not head straight for her but crossed directly to Red Bluff Point. Skirting the frowning cliff we clung to the shore which, however, afforded little protection, being in full view of the dock and cove. Though anyone looking our way could easily have spotted us, there wasn't a soul, so far as we could determine, on or around the boat.

Brian Seaworthy

Headed south, she was fast to the west side of the dock, her port gangplank descending at a steep angle. We could not make out whether the reflection in one of the windows of the dark buildings near the ways was lantern light or the glinting of the moon.

Having taken over the oars, I slowed my strokes so the oarlocks wouldn't squeak. Hardly a breath of air was stirring; the careful dipping of the oars seemed painfully loud as we crossed the *Bennington*'s bow. Upon reaching her stern, Barney climbed over the fantail, making fast the end of the rope ladder we had brought with us. Under other circumstances the spectacle of hoisting up the Parson without a sound would have seemed ludicrous. To steady the boat, to keep the ladder from going under the *Bennington*'s fantail, and finally to raise him over the bulwarks, I pushing and Barney pulling, was almost more than we could manage. This at last accomplished, we made our way on tiptoe along the starboard quarter, through the door, fortunately unlocked, to the recess, through the recess and into

121

the gangway. There was still no evidence of anyone on board. The only sound was a whisper of steam in the engine room, where the gauge showed 45 pounds. I was about to look into the boiler room to see if the fires had been banked, and if not, who was keeping steam, when Barney disappeared around the engine enclosure toward the port gangway.

All of a sudden there was a thud, then the sound of someone falling on the deck. My heart missed a beat, and the Parson's, if his expression was any indication, skipped two or three. Though an icy chill passed through me, I dashed around the engine enclosure to find Barney getting to his feet, and Jib about to hit him again.

"Leave him to me!" grunted Barney, lowering his head and raising his fists. Those little pig-eyes in Jib's sallow face were watching every movement; his bony fists and long sinewy arms were making a peculiar circling motion. Then he swung. The blow was almost too fast to see, but Barney parried it enough so that it glanced off his shoulder. At the same moment he managed an uppercut to Jib's jaw that almost lifted him off the deck. Dazed momentarily, he lunged savagely forward, driving Barney against the low railing above the boiler room with a crash that almost carried him over. But by crouching as he hit and rebounding, Barney was able to land a blow to Jib's chest that brought him to the floor, nearly winded. Barney should not have waited for him to get up. Springing forward and tackling him around the legs, Jib removed him from his feet so suddenly that in twisting around, Barney fell on his ankle. Jib's half smile, upon seeing Barney was in pain and could not rise, indicated that he expected to make mincemeat of me, but I, feinting with my left hand and gathering all my strength in my right, in one lucky blow to his head carried him back against the bulkhead, and down so hard near Barney that he was all but senseless for a few vital moments. On his knees, despite the pain in his ankle, Barney managed to seize Jib's right arm and twist it behind his back, which rendered him completely helpless. For a few moments he showed no distress other than his heavy breathing and I expected he would free himself with some lightning manuever. But as Barney tightened his hold another notch, he winced.

"Why's the boat here?" Barney demanded. "Why're you here?"

"I ain't tellin' you, you sonuvabitch!"

"You ain't?" asked Barney, giving the arm another twist. "That's just a sample. I can do better—like this!"

"AOOW!"

"Why's the boat here?" repeated Barney, forcing Jib's arm a little higher.

"We took her," he gasped, "for . . . for back wages owed."

"Back wages!" I shouted. "*We're* owed the back wages!"

"That Bullard's idea?" asked Barney, "or yours?" Jib threw his head back, gritting his teeth.

"Bullard's." Barney looked at me. We both looked at the Parson. His eyes were bulging out of his head.

"Where's Bullard and the crew?"

"Ashore . . . went ashore."

"When?"

"Half hour ago."

"Now," said Barney, "we'll test your memory. Last year you jimmied the blower valve so Brian couldn't close it, didn't you? DIDN'T YOU!" Jib's head wagged from side to side. "And the *Republic*'s crank indicator—you filed the shaft so it'd break!"

"Gawd . . . OH GAWD! I done it. LEGGO!"

"And loosened this crank so it broke the cylinder!" declared Barney, maintaining his fierce grip. "Bullard told you to, didn't he!" Jib nodded, his eyes closed. "Get some rope," said Barney.

Up to this point all the Parson had indeed supplied was ballast, for he stood with his back against the bulkhead trying to absorb what he was hearing, his hands clasped in front of him, as if prayer might dispel such frightening revelations.

As I tied his ankles and wrists Jib rasped: "I'll kill you bastards!" Whereupon I put a gag around his mouth and neck. Then I helped Barney up. Apparently his ankle was sprained, for he could hardly bear to put his weight on it. Despite this, it was perfectly clear what must be done. We not only had to take the *Bennington* back to the shipyard, we had to run her up on the beach so they couldn't take her back before Captain Hawley and the Chief returned. Motioning to the Parson, I helped Barney into the donkey room where we whispered our plans.

"I can't start the engine on one foot," Barney said. "Do you think you can handle the bar?" I swallowed hard. Could I? I had to. "I'll steer," said Barney, "and Parson, you can shovel coal. Can't you?"

"With the Lord's help," said the Parson, his double chin shaking, "we can do anything!"

"All right. She don't need much coal because she's got 45 pounds on her now. Brian'll show you how to turn on the blower."

After showing the Parson what to do in the boiler room, I helped Barney to the pilot house. There was still no sign of life on shore, except for the light in the shop window which we could now see came from a lantern. We were afraid Bullard was in there.

"After I let the lines go I'll blow twice on the speaking tube," I whispered.

"When we get to the Harbor," Barney said, "she'll have to be goin' fast enough to put her bow up on the sand, but not so fast that we land on your front porch. So when I ring for full astern give her all the soup you can to check her!" I was beginning to shake, appalled at the prospect of running the engine. It was one thing to practice with the Chief and quite another to confront that shiny monster alone.

"You can do it!" Barney insisted, though he would have been just as scared himself. We shook hands solemnly. I went down and quietly let go the stern line, then the bow line. I left the breast line so we could back against it, if necessary, to throw the bow out. On my signal to the boiler room, the Parson was to come up and let that go.

There was no vacuum so I opened the feed water valve. Slowly I barred the engine over until, with a squeal, the vacuum gauge jumped to 10, then right up to 28 inches. The steam had risen to 48 pounds, for I had turned on the blower and showed the Parson how to shut it

Brian Seaworthy

off. With trembling hand I opened the speaking tube and blew twice into it, then took hold of the bar waiting for Barney to ring the bell. The bell rang for slow astern, but I never answered it. Noticing something moving out of the corner of my eye, I turned to the most fearful sight of my life. Holding a long knife that glittered in the lantern light, Jib was standing in the door.

As he jumped forward, I cleared the other doorway in one leap, he hardly two steps behind. By running around one side of the engine enclosure while he was coming around the other, then by reversing direction and racing into the recess and back into one or the other gangways, I managed to keep ahead. I knew I couldn't outguess him for long and was about to race ashore when I noticed that the door to the starboard wheelhouse was ajar. Slipping quickly through it, I crawled up on the plank that bridged the housing just forward of the paddlewheel, inching my way in the darkness to the far corner. Holding my breath as water from the top of the wheelhouse dripped in my hair, I heard Jib pass the heavy iron door, which I hadn't had time to close, then retrace his steps, passing the door again.

Two or three years passed in as many minutes, when the door, its hinges groaning, was suddenly thrown wide open, the flickering light from the gangway illuminating two or three buckets and the far side of the wheelhouse, but not my dark corner. Still holding the knife, Jib looked in, disappeared for a moment, then reappeared with a lantern which, when held up inside, shone full in my face. With those awful eyes fixed upon me, he hung the lantern on a wheel bolt, put the knife between his teeth, and climbed on a paddle bucket. As he crawled toward me, Barney's face suddenly appeared in the door. Jib by this time was out of his reach, and his bad ankle would not permit him to follow. I had thought of jumping into the water but to do so now I would have to step within striking distance of the knife. I think I was about to faint.

Suddenly the great wheel began

to turn. The lantern plummeted into the water and Jib lost his balance. Struggling to regain it he swung his arm around still holding on to the knife, which stuck on a paddle bucket, penetrating half an inch into the oak. Pitching forward with a scream he plunged below headfirst, bucket after bucket following him into the foam. Drenched to the skin I clung to my narrow perch as the wheel made two complete revolutions with the knife still stuck in the paddle bucket. I could not and did not move so much as a finger.

The wheel stopped turning. Gradually aware that I was safe, I sidestepped along the plank inch by inch. I reached the bulkhead door. Barney pulled me through.

"Praise God!" exclaimed the Parson raising his arms, then throwing them around our shoulders. Barney was peering down for the slightest sign of Jib around or near the wheel. There was none. I shuddered to think I would have been there if he had not.

"May the Lord preserve even his dark soul!" intoned the Parson.

"Just pray we can get out of here," declared Barney. "It's us that need preservin'!"

Standing up to the engine after my frightful ordeal in the wheelhouse seemed an utter impossibility. Physically, at least, Barney was even in worse shape, having hobbled from the pilot house and borne down on his painful ankle to turn the engine over. But our determination rallied as I again helped him up the stairs. No one prevented us now from carrying out our plans, though we could hardly believe that the engine room bell, the turning of the wheels, or Jib's scream hadn't been heard on shore —if anyone was there to hear.

Hurriedly dispatching the agitated Parson to the boiler room, I resumed my station before the engine. Shakily I responded to Barney's two bells and jingler: slow astern. This threw the bow out, since the breast line was still fast to the dock. The Parson had just come up from the boiler room to let it go, as planned, when I heard an alarming shout. Running out on deck I saw our doom trundling along the dock toward the gangplank as fast as his fat legs would propel him, with three roustabouts right behind. The first frantic thing that came into my head was to uncleat the breast line and let it go, but in the absence of any wind this accomplished nothing. Though no longer tied to the dock the boat stayed right where she was, her bow and forward quarter slightly out, yet not far enough but what the gangplank still reached ashore. Barney, on one leg outside the pilot house, looked as though the jig was finally up. It was the Parson who rallied now, drawing himself up to his full height at the head of the gangplank.

"*In the name of the Lord* you are forbidden to step one foot on this boat!" he commanded, his double chin emphasizing every word.

"Out of my way!" puffed Bullard, his three henchmen directly behind. I am sure that no petition in the name of the Lord was ever answered more quickly or from a more unlikely source. As if the heavens had opened, a powerful jet of water from above struck Bullard full in the face. Looking up I beheld—of all conceivable deliverers (it never occurred to me that she had remained aboard)—Gussie on the bridge grasping the nozzle of the fire hose with all the strength she possessed.

"Take that, you stack of blubber!" she shrilled. The impact was such that in letting go of the hand rails of the gangplank to protect his face, Bullard lost his footing, tumbled backward, and went down on the dock like a sack of meal, Gussie all the while playing the hose over his whole length and back again. When the roustabouts tried to help him, she drenched them so forcefully that they had no recourse but to turn their backs and clamber out of the way.

The gangplank barely reached from the dock to the guard. With a little heaving the Parson and I were able to shove it into the water. I then raced back to the engine room, entering the door just as Barney rang the bell. The crank indicator crept toward 3 o'clock. My hands shook and my teeth fairly rattled as I grasped the bar and pulled it down. Down rushed the crosshead and piston rod. Up on the bar. Up they went. Down. Down they dropped, swiftly. Up.

Down. On the fourth upstroke I reached with my left hand for the handle controlling the eccentrics, and with one eye on the paddle indicator, pulled it down. KLUNK! The great engine took hold! For a few moments I couldn't let go of the bar, my knees shook so.

Then the bell rang for full ahead. The throttle was retarded, and as I pulled it down the massive engine answered with powerful strokes of the great crank. Temporarily, at least, fear had succumbed to the triumphant thrill of victory over the engine. Hurrying into the donkey room to look out of the window, I saw from landmarks still lighted by the moon that we were already half way to the shipyard. The slow bell sounded within a minute after my return to the engine. I closed the throttle. The stop bell rang. I disconnected the eccentrics and shut off the water to the condenser. Though the engine had ceased to breathe, it was still turning over from the momentum of the paddlewheels. As I opened the throttle wide, which was always done when operating with the bar, my shaking returned in

129

full measure. Momentarily I would have to check the engine and execute the frightful maneuver of reversing it while the boat was still moving rapidly forward.

Two bells. Hard astern! When the paddle indicator came around to 9 o'clock, I breathlessly came down on the bar. The indicator reversed direction. When it drifted over the bottom center, I came up hard with both hands. Down! Up! Down! Just as the stop bell rang, I felt the bow hit the sand. With a great scrunch we were lifted upward, upward, until we ground to a halt. I was still holding on to the bar, my knees knocking, my eyes closed, the sweat dripping over my eyelids, when the speaking tube whistled. The gong rang with abandon, the jingler, and then the bell on top of the pilot house. Finally the whistle boomed a joyous salute.

Opening my eyes at last and releasing the bar, I beheld Gussie's toothless grin in the doorway. "Ain't it too bad Cap'n Seaworthy can't see you now!"

"Chip off the old block, ain't he!" said Barney in the other door-way. Then he danced a one-legged jig in the gangway.

CHAPTER

In Which Some Persons

Get Their Just Deserts

And Others Have Cake

THE BOW OF THE BENNINGTON came to rest within twenty feet of the back porch of the rooming house. Climbing down to the beach, we saw that the paddle-wheels were almost out of water. The boat was safe from her enemies; the question now was whether she could be removed even by her friends.

"What on earth happened?" exclaimed Mrs. Mayberry, hurrying down the bank. "Merciful Heavens!"

"Were Heaven not merciful we'd have been at the mercy of Bullard!" declared the Parson.

"Brian run the engine like a veteran!" Gussie announced. "And Barney don't have nothin' to learn 'bout steerin'!"

"We'd all be in the chain locker if it wa'n't for Gussie," said Barney. "She aims a mighty mean hose! Bullard got real damp! And guess who fired! The Parson!"

"I've a much clearer idea of purgatory than before I became a fireman!" acknowledged the Parson, brushing ashes from around his collar. There being no need to secure the *Bennington* with lines, we all went up to the house while Mrs. Mayberry strapped up Barney's sprained ankle. Upon hearing of our fight and Jib's demise under the wheel, she turned as white as the kitchen curtains.

"If ever a life was sacrificed in self-defense, this was it. I saw the whole terrible thing, and shall so testify!" affirmed the Parson as solemnly as if this were Judgment Day.

The bell and whistle having aroused the farmers and brought them to the shipyard, we were back on the beach at sunup and still there at church time. The Parson's sermon was never delivered; he refused to leave until the Captain and Chief returned, which they did late in the afternoon. Uncle arrived soon after, having taken the ferry from Cumberland Head and the stage from Grand Isle.

"I always thought Bullard was as two-faced as a double-bitted axe!" declared the Chief. "And as crooked as a corkscrew to boot!" Uncle's face was very red.

"I could have staked my life on his honesty. Apparently Captain Seaworthy never found fault with him."

"He never found much to praise, either," testified Captain Hawley. "He was waiting for a chance to replace him."

"I certainly owe you gentlemen an apology—and you boys, too. Imagine being led to believe the accidents last summer were due to negligence!"

"It's just as Mr. Burnside said, Uncle Reuel. Captain Bullard has been putting money in his pocket for every ton of clinker coal we've burned. And I'll bet that's not all he's taken!"

"Unfortunately he has been handling all receipts and disbursements himself. He has also been borrowing money in the Company's name. This I discovered only last week when he asked me to secure another temporary loan in Plattsburg. I was not successful in this. I'm afraid the blame is largely mine. I appointed him marine su-

pervisor and have been altogether too trusting."

"It's not your fault," said Mrs. Mayberry, patting Uncle's hand. "How would you know you were dealing with a crook?"

"By examining receipts and expenditures. That I can assure you I will do from now on."

The Chief pointed at the *Bennington*. "He'd've even lifted *her* if it wa'n't for the boys."

Uncle shook his head. "I can't believe he'd get away with that in a court of law."

"A ship may be attached by the crew or others if payments for services or wages are in arrears," explained the Captain. "No doubt he thought if he took her he could keep her. Possession is nine points of the law."

"We must notify the authorities about Jib at once. Is there a possibility he might have survived?"

"Not a chance under that wheel," Barney told Uncle. "We couldn't find a trace of him."

"A dreadful thing!" declared Uncle, removing his breast-pocket handkerchief and mopping his face and neck. "Do you think you'll have trouble refloating the *Bennington*?"

"She'd dig herself out with more of her wheels in the water," said the Captain. "If she can't we'll pull her off with the *Republic*. We'll take the rowboat and see how much of her is aground." Suddenly I remembered tying the rowboat to her stern in Mark's Bay. It was still intact but half full of water and I nearly fell overboard bringing it around. The *Bennington* proving to be at least half afloat, the Captain and Chief thought that with enough ballast aft we might get her off without the *Republic*.

Hitching Agatha to the Parson's carriage the next morning, Barney and I called on everyone we could find all the way to the village. We were able to round up nearly two hundred, or roughly a ton-and-a-half, of people, the minimum the Captain thought we needed for ballast. With a full head of steam and the Chief on the bar, with Mr. Mc-Gettrick, Ashes Robarge, Barney and I at the trimming barrels on the cross deck, and the Parson's large flock in the recess, the stern, and as far aft as they could get in the hall upstairs, all was ready at three o'clock. When the whistle blew, the Chief gave the engine all it had; we started rolling the barrels back and forth, and the Parson's army in the stern began singing *The Battle Hymn of the Republic*, tramping in unison from port to starboard and starboard to port. Now a little deeper in the water on one side and now on the other as the ballast shifted, the thrashing wheels clawed tons of water shoreward, inundating the beach clear to the bow. Slowly but inexorably she began to move, until suddenly we were free of the sand. A cheer went up as we landed at the wharf. The Captain then opened the bar and tapped several kegs of Jamaica rum, which more than compensated the volunteers for what, after all, had been a pleasant interlude.

It turned out that there wasn't a penny in the treasury to have paid this multitude. In order to satisfy some of our creditors and to purchase coal and supplies we had to sell the *Gloria*. I was in tears when she steamed away but consoled myself that her sacrifice was a noble one. Since prospects to pay wages in arrears were dim, I proposed that part ownership in the Company be transferred to Captain Hawley, the Chief, Barney, Chief DuFour, Mrs. Mayberry, Gussie, Mr. McGettrick, Ashes Robarge, and several others who were willing to wait. Uncle was against this, saying it just wasn't done, but I insisted they had as much of a stake in a cloudy future as we. Steps were accordingly taken to apportion a third of the stock according to their importance and the number of years they had served.

So much happened during the next weeks that we were hard put to run the boats and attend hearings on shore. To no one's surprise, Bullard became captain of the *Defiance*, which confirmed our suspicion that in running the *Republic* at two-thirds' speed and hauling out the *Bennington* to remove her from service he had been part of the opposition all along. But we were shocked that Chief DuFour would go with him as engineer. Despite my argument that he had been threatened or intimidated into doing this, his name had to be removed from those who were to receive stock in the Company.

No charges resulted from Jib's death, which was ruled justifiable homicide. (His body floated up not far from the Mark's Bay wharf.) Bullard denied everything Jib had admitted, and otherwise covered his tracks so carefully that there was not yet enough evidence to bring an indictment. The State's Attorney explained to Uncle that if he were to impanel a grand jury which could not find a true bill against Bullard, he could never again be indicted. The lawyers and sheriffs argued for days about his seizure of the *Bennington* and our taking it back without licenses. The newspapers were so full of rumors that even our own employees hardly knew what to believe.

If there was one bright spot it was Mr. Burnside's confidence in the future. Upon receipt of a long letter from us, he wired that he would provide an unlimited amount of coal on credit, which happily allowed us to take care of other needs. A retired Isle La Motte captain and an elderly engineer from Vergennes having agreed to run

the *Bennington* until replacements were found, Captain Hawley, the Chief, Barney, Gussie, and I returned to the *Republic*. Uncle later became purser, Mrs. Mayberry followed as stewardess, and Mr. McGettrick as freight clerk. Thus we continued through the fall, living so nearly from hand to mouth that the principal of the academy had to excuse me on Fridays so I could contribute free labor on weekends. Keeping the boilers clean fortunately proved to be only half the work with Mr. Burnside's coal. Moreover, we burned much less of it per hour, as he had promised.

More because of competition than despite it, the *Republic* became the happiest of boats. As swift at full throttle as the *Defiance*, she often beat her because her pilot had departed and Bullard was awkward getting in and out of small landings. However, since the *Defiance* had recently gained a reputation as the faster boat and therefore a large share of the business, he could afford to skip small landings, while we felt obliged to stop at every one. With our rates cut to the bone, we needed every penny we earned, and more, particularly in late fall and early winter when business fell off.

It is as characteristic of ships as of people that weeks, months, even years pass without remarkable incident, until a day comes which changes everything that has gone before and everything to come. While my first two years afloat had hardly been without incident they paled by comparison with a lowering December Saturday that began in Whitehall. Uncle was working in his stateroom and I had just come up from the boiler room for air.

"I don't like the smell of this wind!" declared the Chief.

"Why not?"

"It's shiftin' to the east. And the sky looks greasier'n a tub of tallow. My bunion aches, and that ain't a good sign, either. Well, it don't matter. The *Republic* can take anythin' the elements dish out." It being but a few minutes to sailing time he went below to check his auxiliaries, while I watched the clammy wind edge the flag around to the southwest as the last of some thirty passengers hurried aboard.

From the cross deck I could see that the *Defiance* was getting no more business than we.

Our last arrival, in a wheel chair, was a slight middle-aged man with an expressive face and iron-grey hair. After a deckhand rolled his chair up the gangplank, the man tucked the cane he was carrying between his knees, opened his purse and gave him a coin. They talked for a moment, the deckhand turned and pointed at me, and the man smiled. He was just starting to propel his chair toward me and I, thinking he wanted something, had taken my first step toward him, when Uncle appeared from the forward hatchway. The stranger's eyes started from their sockets. Grasping the arm of the wheel chair with one hand and his cane with the other, he pushed himself to his feet.

"THIEF! PIRATE! MURDERER!" Uncle's ruddy face turned oyster-grey. "SEIZE HIM! HE'S A CRIMINAL!" cried the stranger, brandishing his cane. Everyone within hearing was too shocked to act—everyone but Uncle. Dodging past the stranger and down the gang-

plank, he ran along the dock as if propelled from a slingshot, never looking back until he had reached the *Defiance*, the stranger still shouting: "STOP THAT MAN! STOP HIM!"

"Who do you think you are!" I demanded. "Do you know who that man is?"

"*Know who he is!*" exclaimed the stranger. "That man is the biggest swindler that ever walked in a pair of shoes! He took every penny I owned!" I was convinced the stranger was out of his head.

"That man happens to be my uncle!" I said defiantly.

"*Your uncle!*" He banged his cane on the deck. "That man is Jacob Dugan! Where does that boat go?"

"Burlington." Calming down a bit but breathing heavily and never taking his eyes from me, the stranger eased himself back into his chair.

"Brian Seaworthy." I was surprised he could know my name; I had never laid eyes on him.

"You're a picture of your mother." He stretched out his hands to take mine, but I would not offer

them. He did not seem offended; indeed his face softened as he looked steadfastly into mine.

"I am your Uncle Reuel." The bewildering impact of these words, the emotion that suffused my entire being, can more readily be imagined than expressed. I felt sick. I felt as if Father had died again and I was alone in a hostile world. I was no more prepared to accept this uncle than to reject the other, whose identity, despite his distant manner and his mistakes, I had never doubted. Neither had the authorities who had appointed him conservator of Father's estate. Yet this man's earnest face compelled me to believe he was telling the truth.

Unbuttoning his overcoat and reaching into his pocket he withdrew a small leather case, taking from it a daguerreotype, which he handed to me. Three faces appeared on it: Father's as a young man, Mother's, unmistakably, and the other? I looked from the picture to the stranger and back again.

"A much younger face, but mine, is it not?" There could be no question. "It was taken on their wedding day." Tears welled into his eyes. This time, as he stretched out his hands, I took them. I could not smile or speak; I could not even think.

"It is too much for you. It is too much for me. Let me engage a stateroom where we can talk. Where is the purser's office?"

"Uncle . . . I mean, he was the purser," I mumbled. He raised his hands, holding them high above his head.

"Dear God! I hope there's something left in the treasury!" The whistle blew and the gangplank rumbled over the cross deck.

"I have to go down to the boiler room," I said, wheeling him into the gangway. "I'll be back."

"I'll wait here. Thank you. Don't hurry." I backed down the ladder to the boiler room two rungs at a time.

"What's the matter?" asked Barney. "Seen a spook, or somethin'?"

"Yes."

"Wha'd'ya mean?"

"There's a man upstairs, just came aboard in a wheel chair . . . he's my Uncle Reuel, he says. He's got a picture showing Father and

Mother, and he's in it." Barney was dumbfounded.

"He's *what!*"

"He's Uncle Reuel. He *is!*" It was one of the few times I ever saw Barney almost at a loss for words.

"What about your . . . your other uncle?"

"He's gone. He ran away. He's on the *Defiance*. His real name is Dugan!"

"Go see Father and the Captain, and get Ashes to fire for you," said Barney upon recovering his equilibrium. I went back up and wheeled Uncle Reuel to the door of the engine room. When the Chief came out I said:

"This is my Uncle Reuel."

"Your *what?*" said the Chief. But that was the extent of his surprise. Upon learning what had happened he merely said, "I always thought Dugan was crooked as a dog's hind leg. But what could I say?"

"Dugan," Uncle revealed, "was my partner. When I discovered he'd fleeced me I had a seizure and for months was nearer dead than alive. He supposed I would never recover. Since he knew all about the Seaworthys, your father's death presented him with the tailor-made opportunity of impersonating me. Oh, I tell you he's the slickest and most diabolical operator in the country. I just pray he hasn't stolen you blind!''

"We still have our shirts," said the Chief, "but that's about all." The lines across Uncle's forehead, arching over his eyes, were deeply etched with fatigue. He said he would like to rest if we didn't mind, and I wheeled him to the door of a stateroom on the main deck. The chair was too wide to go through and he walked in with his cane, though none too steadily.

The news raced through the boat like a prairie fire. On my way to the pilot house I saw Mrs. Mayberry standing outside by the rail behind the stairs to the hurricane deck. She was crying. I saw her look at her engagement ring, take it off her finger and draw her hand back as if she were going to throw it into the lake. Instead she put it in her purse. I did not think anything I could say would help, so I quietly withdrew and climbed the stairs on the opposite side.

If the Captain was shocked at this latest upheaval he did not have much more than the Chief to say about it. He was one of the least excitable men I ever knew, which was one reason he was captain.

"That's too bad," he said. "But don't worry. We'll make it somehow."

By the time we had warped around the Elbow, the northern sky was darkening though the wind seemed to have let up a little. It rose again after we left Ticonderoga, not steadily but in fits and starts. The grey-black crescent from north to east now occupied a third of the sky.

"We're in for something," the Captain said, ringing the deck bell. "Close all the hatches," he ordered the first mate, "and take down the flags."

"I'll help," I said, glad to do something but pore over my afflictions.

"You'd better stay here; I'll need a quartermaster when we get to Split Rock."

He was right. Having dispensed with our pilot for the sake of economy, the Captain had been doing

141

much of the steering himself, but no man could handle the wheel alone in a storm. This wind, after it made up its mind, blew with sharply rising intensity straight out of the north, hitting us head on. The barometer stood barely above 28. Since it was snowing when we reached Westport and our visibility was growing less by the minute, the Captain thought perhaps we ought to stay there. But when Bullard blew the whistle to leave, the Captain said we surely were up to it if the *Defiance* was.

The wind rose frightfully as we rounded Steam Mill Point, spewing gusts of snow across the forward promenade. Momentarily leaving the wheel to me, the Captain whistled down to the Chief: "We'll go on compass." Several times each summer we practiced our compass courses which had been plotted from one end of the lake to the other. Since the distance between two points had to be run in exactly so many minutes, steam was always cut from 53 to 40 pounds, the lower pressure being much easier to maintain precisely. For if the pressure varied as

much as a pound, so did the number of revolutions of the wheels per minute and, in turn, the distance covered. The importance of proper calculations in a fog so thick that in a thirty-mile run not a single lighthouse, point, or island could be seen, is evident; once we could not even find the Plattsburg breakwater when, having almost completed our compass course, we stopped a thousand feet from the entrance and were guided in by the bell on the jetty.

We had been on compass only a few minutes when we could hardly see the *Defiance* off to port; at times we could not even see the flagstaff on our own bow. The wind whipped the whitecaps off the waves and the lanyards drummed against the flagstaffs. The guy wires moaned and the windows rattled. Shrouded in driving snow, the creaking pilot house no longer seemed part of the boat.

"This is heavy as anything I ever saw," said the Captain, his eyes straining from the compass to the bow. "We'll really catch it at Split Rock."

"I don't see the *Defiance*," I said.

Brian Seaworthy

"He's running in the lee of the mountain, but there isn't much lee in this wind. Better to breast the sea and have some elbow room." Breast it we did. The bow no sooner plunged into one trough than the next wave was upon it; every so often it barely rose in time, or so it seemed. I wondered how we would fare ahead beyond the point when totally in the grip of this roaring Canadian wind. Seafarers little understand the fury of thirty miles of open fresh water. I had heard of storms which the lake's largest vessels could not weather; Captain Hawley remembered one which snapped the paddleshaft of an early steamer, and another in which he thought he would land on the roof of the freight shed. If he was worried today he did not let on. As immaculately unruffled as usual, his expression of vigilance contained also a certain serene confidence in the amount of punishment the *Republic* could withstand.

The way the sea was running he presumed the Split Rock lighthouse was now just off our larboard bow. We were about to change our bearing when a loud report like an explosion, though much longer, pierced the shrieking wind. I had never heard such a dreadful sound; even the Captain looked shocked and alarmed. My first thought was that a boiler had gone up, but the *Republic* never faltered. Suddenly, in a momentary break in the blizzard, we saw the stern of the *Defiance* to port.

"Hard 'a starboard!" commanded the Captain, ringing the stop bell. As we tugged on the big wheel with all our strength, I shifted my position to the side so I could pull on the upper handles and stand on the lower rungs for leverage. The bow came gradually around until the wind caught it, wheeling us swiftly to starboard. The engine had stopped, but the gale was driving us south half as fast as if we had sails.

"They must have hit the cliff! They're backing off!" The Captain rang for slow astern so that we would be south of, and parallel to, the *Defiance* whose outline appeared, disappeared, and appeared again in the swirling snow.

"Her bow is all stove in!" I exclaimed. The Captain rang for general quarters.

"The *Defiance* hit the cliff!" he shouted to the Chief through the speaking tube. "Stand by for lowering the starboard lifeboats!" Within two minutes the deckhands were swarming over the boats in the stinging snow, throwing off the covers, hauling on the lines, and swinging out the davits. We were now directly in the lee of the *Defiance* and broadside to her, though she was headed west and we east. Being on the windward side, she gradually closed the gap until she wasn't more than seventy-five feet away, listing distinctly toward the bow.

"There's a hole the size of a moose in her bow!" declared the Captain, squinting through his spy glass. "If her bulkheads are open she's a goner!" One of her port lifeboats was being lowered. When it was almost down it rose in the air again as the *Defiance* rolled to starboard, then settled safely in the water. Two of our own boats were on their way around our stern.

"God above!" cried the Captain, training his glass on the *Defiance's*

lifeboat. "Bullard and Dugan are the only ones in it!" Picking up the other glass I saw an unspeakable scene: with his clamoring passengers on deck, Bullard was hacking with a knife at the falls still fastened to the lifeboat. The moment it was free he took to one oar and Dugan to the other; then they began pulling away for all they were worth, disappearing among the crests just as our boat arrived. The muscles in the Captain's cheeks were working over his clenched jaws; putting down his glass he watched our deckhands fighting for headway in the violent sea. As I trained my glass on the second of the *Defiance's* lifeboats, with ten or fifteen passengers milling around it on the hurricane deck, I distinctly made out the figure of Chief Du-Four, now in command, running back and forth to line up the people, and shouting to the deckhands manning the falls. As soon as the boat was loaded, swung out, and on the way down, he appeared on the main deck forward, aft, and amidships, shouting to the hands in our lifeboats and directing his own crew as they rolled out three rope ladders. Heavily down by the bow, the *Defiance* was beginning to wallow and to roll sluggishly as the water in her forward compartments sloshed from side to side.

The following sea swiftly bore her lifeboat around our stern under the leeward guard, where its fifteen passengers safely climbed a rope ladder to the cross deck. It was pulling away for another load just as our two crowded boats left the *Defiance*, now filling so fast that her guards dipped into the water every time she rolled. I could count only ten people, with Chief DuFour, left aboard her. By the time the first lifeboat returned, she was down so deep that rope ladders were no longer necessary; every time she listed to port, two or three were able to climb in directly from the main deck. The Chief was the last to leave, and none too soon; the *Defiance* was rolling so far and staying so long that it seemed she must soon turn over.

But she did not. As the last lifeboat rounded our stern, her bow went down, her wheels came out of water, her stern slowly lifted her rudder completely into the air. There she hung for a few awful moments, then down she plunged window by window, a cloud of steam pouring out of her turtle deck above her walking beam. She sank with a muffled roar amidst geysers of steam and water. As we backed away, only a few life preservers and a flagstaff bearing the gilded antlers of a moose tossed above her grave in four hundred feet of water.

For years thereafter, the *Defiance* sank again and again in my worst and best dreams, dwarfing the details of the rest of our trip home. The waves were so high as they burst over the bow, advancing in walls over the cross deck, that the deckhands had to jump up and hold on to the pipes fastened to the carlings. Mr. McGettrick found seventeen hundred dollars in an envelope under the mattress in Uncle Reuel's—I mean Dugan's—stateroom. Nothing was ever heard from him and Bullard. Their overturned lifeboat was found on a beach around the point from Split Rock. We supposed they might have made it ashore, in which case

Chief Barnaby hoped the rattle-snakes on the mountain had given them a good reception.

Freed from Bullard, who had threatened dire consequences if he did not serve on the *Defiance*, Chief DuFour, with new-found confidence born of his exertions, was the hero of the hour. I fired with Ashes Robarge most of the way back. Not quite comprehending all that had happened, he reverted to his favorite subject: "These pretty good boilers, but you take the iron in Old Bess . . ."

The boats ended their season shortly afterward and I continued the monotony of my classes, broken early one Tuesday afternoon when the principal excused me for the rest of the day, saying I was wanted at the shipyard. Unable to find a soul in the shops, I had just entered the house when a chorus of voices shouted: "SURPRISE!" and the living room was suddenly full of the people who meant everything to me. Mr. McGettrick appeared with a huge punch bowl and Gussie bore in not one birthday cake but two, with the *Republic* and *Bennington* expertly fashioned on top.

147

Mr. Burnside was there, full of smiles and optimism, vowing to bring Jeanie and her father north on a boatman's tour in the spring.

From the moment the party began, the conspicuous absence of Barney and the Chief intruded on my fun.

"Where are Barney and the Chief?" I finally asked the Parson.

"Ask me no questions and I'll tell you no lies!" he declared solemnly, his double chin shaking. Just then a familiar whistle blew in the bay. Rushing out on the porch, I beheld the *Gloria* steaming regally in with the Chief at the wheel, and Barney standing on her bow with the widest of his grins. I did not learn until later that they all had to dig pretty deep to get her back; one particularly helpful item having been the solitaire in Mrs. Mayberry's engagement ring.

They all stayed well into the evening and we had a rare time. After they had gone, Uncle Reuel, who under Mrs. Mayberry's care had almost abandoned his wheel chair, remained in the kitchen reading the paper. When I went out in the hall on my way down to

look the *Gloria* over, I saw Mrs. Mayberry arranging her hair in front of the mirror.

The *Gloria* proved as fit as the day we sold her, and the big boats, while they could use a little paint here and there, never looked better. I climbed to the *Republic's* pilot house which was serving its usual role as winter quarters for dozens of flies; then I went down through the stateroom hall pausing at the top of the stairs to decide whether at seventeen I was too old to slide down the banister. I did not think I was.

Stopping at the engine room to look at the machinery, it came over me that I had done the same thing under the same circumstances before, which indeed I had. The engine was covered with whale oil, but when the whistle blew in the spring the brightwork would again be as shiny, the Chief would say, "as a Christian's eyeball."

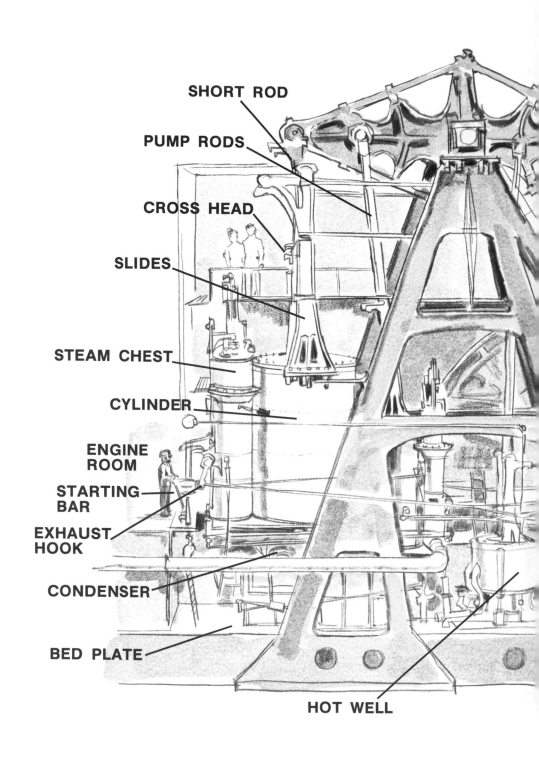

SHORT ROD

PUMP RODS

CROSS HEAD

SLIDES

STEAM CHEST

CYLINDER

ENGINE
ROOM

STARTING
BAR

EXHAUST
HOOK

CONDENSER

BED PLATE

HOT WELL

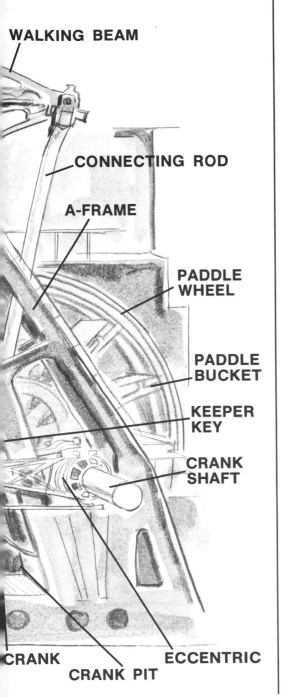

WALKING BEAM

CONNECTING ROD

A-FRAME

PADDLE WHEEL

PADDLE BUCKET

KEEPER KEY

CRANK SHAFT

CRANK

CRANK PIT

ECCENTRIC

Diagram of engine of the

REPUBLIC

THE SIMPLEST, THE MOST ENDURING and spectacular of marine steam engines was the vertical beam, aptly named for its great height, and for the walking beam which transferred power from the piston to the connecting rod, crank, and paddlewheels.

The steam chests admitted low pressure steam from the boilers to the very large single cylinder by way of an ingenious valve mechanism, which also exhausted the spent steam down into the condenser, there to be transformed to a vacuum. Thus while steam was pushing one end of the piston, vacuum was pulling the other.

The ritual of the engineer starting, stopping, and backing the engine by raising and lowering the starting bar which controlled the valve gear and set in motion a great mechanism as tall as a three story building, struck generations of travelers with wonder.

151

This book was designed
by John R. Scotford, Jr.

Set in Bell type by
The Stinehour Press,
Lunenburg, Vermont,

it was printed on
special Nimrod paper
by The Nimrod Press,
Boston, Massachusetts,

and bound there by
The Stanhope Bindery.

DATE DUE

NO11 95			
NO20 95			
Nov 24			
12/1/95			

DEMCO 38-297